AN EVANS NOVEL OF THE WEST

COLFAX

ROBERT J. CONLEY

M. EVANS & COMPANY, INC.   NEW YORK

Library of Congress Cataloging-in-Publication Data

Conley, Robert J.

   Colfax / Robert J. Conley
      p.   cm.—(An Evans novel of the West)
   ISBN 0-87131-559-9
   I. Title.   II. Series.
PS3553.0494C65 1989 88-38750
813'.54—dc19

M. Evans and Company, Inc.
216 East 49 Street
New York, New York 10017

Manufactured in the United States of America

9 8 7 6 5 4 3 2 1

Chapter One

Luton rode slowly. He was in no hurry, had no destination really in mind, and there was no place he had to be. He just wanted to get away from town, away from people, wanted some time to himself to think. He rode east toward the hills, enjoying the feel of the strong movements of the mare beneath him. It had been some time since he'd been in a saddle.

Life's just too damn easy, he thought, and he wondered why he had allowed it to get that way. Too damn soft. There was something on his mind, but he couldn't seem to focus his thoughts on it. It was in there somewhere, all mixed up with a bunch of other thoughts. Maybe it wasn't even a thought, not a real thought, just a kind of feeling, a vague feeling, an uneasiness that had set in and had been nagging at him now for some while. He urged the mare up the side of the hill, liking the slight sense of work involved in even that small effort. On top, where the ground leveled off, he stopped in the tall prairie grass and dismounted.

A slight breeze was causing the grasses to roll across the sides of the hills and on down into the valley and across it toward the river like ocean waves. It was a pleasant Iowa summer day, and out away from town, Luton suddenly felt good. From where he stood, he could look over the whole town of Riddle. He could even make out the river bridge that crossed the Missouri, leading into the neighboring town of West Riddle, Nebraska. This place had been his home for a long time. A good many years, he thought.

He sat down in the grass, still holding the reins to the mare loosely in his hands. Maybe too many. At least enough. The thought had formed, and he had expressed it to himself so easily and naturally that it had come as a surprise. That was the source of the uneasy feeling he had been carrying around with him. He was tired of the job at Riddle. He was tired of Iowa.

It does get too damn cold up here in the winter, he thought, at least for an old Texas boy. The job had been too easy for too long. Luton had made that discovery eight years earlier when he had taken a trip to Texas to seek out the murderers of his younger brother. He had found that he winded too easily. He wasn't as alert as he used to be, nor as quick. Being town marshal of Riddle all those years had made him soft, and for years that had been just fine with him. The war, a few years of manhunting, and a career as a town-taming lawman, ending with the cleaning up of Riddle, had been enough action for one lifetime. He had settled into the comfort of the job easily and gratefully, a comfort that he, himself, had created, and his resulting complacency had been seriously interrupted only once—the time he had gone back to Texas.

Recalling that episode in his life made him think of the strange man, Colfax, the hired killer who had drawn a bead on him and then let him go. Yes, he thought, he had grown soft. Colfax could have killed him that day eight years ago. He was lucky that Bud's murderers had gotten what they deserved. Luck. That was all it had been. Just luck. Then he thought of Emily.

Emily. Could Emily be in back of all this? His thoughts about Emily? Yes, by God, he said to himself. Of course. It's Emily. It had been Emily all along. She was the finest woman he had ever met. He had realized that almost from the beginning, from the

2

time he had first met her on the train going to Texas. Yes, he was bored with his job, tired of Iowa, and he wanted Emily. Meeting Emily had been the one really good thing to come out of the Texas trip. Oh, in a way it had been good to see Will again, but that wasn't the same. Will had been in trouble. They had had to fight to regain Will's ranch.

Luton never forgot that his old friend Will Milam had made him an offer. He had actually offered Luton a partnership, half of his ranch, if Luton would move back to Texas. He would resign his position as town marshal of Riddle, Iowa, leave Iowa for good, move back to Texas where he really belonged, take Will Milam up on his offer, and settle down with Emily. And he had better get after it, he thought, because he sure as hell wasn't getting any younger.

He stood up and started to mount the mare, but a new thought made him pause. Would Will's offer still be good? The offer had been made almost immediately after Will's ranch had been restored to him with Luton's help. Eight years had gone by since then. Eight long years. People change their minds. Luton had. Maybe Will had, too. And what about Emily? Luton had never spoken to her of marriage, had never said anything to her concerning his feelings for her. Maybe she had remarried. Or perhaps those feelings were not mutual. Luton couldn't come up with any reason why they should be, no matter how hard he searched his mind. He had only a few dollars to his name, and he sure wasn't young anymore. Even young, he hadn't been much to look at, he thought. And then there was the boy, Matt. He'd be about fifteen by now, Luton guessed. He marveled at how casually he had let the years race through his life. His earlier enthusiasm began to wane as he climbed back up into the saddle. He sat for a moment; his mare was puzzled, wondering what he was up to.

"By damn," he said, "there's only one way I'm ever going to find out. Come on. Let's go, old girl."

The mare began to pick her way cautiously down the steep hillside, sensibly resisting Luton's impatient urgings to her to hurry.

He was anxious to get back to his office in town. She was concerned with staying on all fours. As the grade eased out somewhat, they picked up a little speed, and by the time they reached level ground, the mare was moving along at a good trot. Rounding a small clump of trees, rider and horse were both startled. Luton hauled back on the reins and shouted. "Whoa. Ho, up there."

The mare reared, causing Luton to have to fight a bit to stay on her back. Then she settled down. There in the path before them were two mounted men. Luton recognized Victor Bragg, the president of the Riddle Valley Bank. The other man, almost as well dressed as the banker, was a stranger to Luton. It seemed a little out of the ordinary for the banker to be having a conference on horseback out away from town like this, but a quick second thought told Luton that old tight-fisted Bragg was probably trying to sell the man some real estate. Luton, himself, had very nearly bought a place from Bragg some years ago. At the last minute he had decided against it, backed out of the deal, and kept his little rental house on the edge of town. It was a good thing, too, he thought, the way things were working out. It would be a whole hell of a lot easier to ride away from Riddle without having to get rid of property.

"Howdy, Victor," he said.

"Good morning, Sarge," said the banker, a dour expression on his face, in spite of the fact that he had familiarly used Bluff Luton's wartime nickname. "Sorry to run up on you like that. I didn't expect anyone to be out here."

"That's all right," said Bragg.

Luton hesitated a moment longer, half expecting an introduction to the stranger. When it became obvious that none was forthcoming, he touched the brim of his hat and nodded.

"Well," he said, "I'll be on my way. Good day, gentlemen."

"Good day," said Bragg, just a bit brusquely, thought Luton. The stranger nodded. Luton rode on toward town wondering what the men were up to out there. The unexpectedness of the scene brought out of him the suspicious nature of the lawman. He

4

reminded himself that he was contemplating leaving all that behind him. They could talk out there if they wanted to. It was none of his damn business, anyhow. Bragg could be a surly bastard when he wanted to be, so there was really nothing unusual about his behavior. Likely they had been startled by Luton, just as old Bragg had been about to name a money figure. By the time he was back in his office, he had put the whole incident out of his mind.

He wadded up a piece of paper and threw it toward the wastebasket. It missed and landed on the floor. He laid out a fresh one, dipped the pen into the inkwell, and started over again. He wrote May 19, 1882, again at the top of the sheet, then a new greeting.

Dear Mrs. Fisher,
    Well, I guess that little Matthew is just about growed up by now.

He reread the sentence, tore up the paper and threw it after the other one. He started again. Finally he began with an explanation for not having written earlier. Then he wrote some more, hesitating only when he got to the difficult part of the letter. Then he read this part out loud, to see if it made sense.

Well that is not what I am writing this letter to you about anyway. I am just rambling on trying to get up the courage and find the right words to say what it is that I want to say. Mrs. Fisher. . . . Emily. You are certainly one of the finest women I have ever known. Before I left Texas way back then I thought about asking you to come with me back to Iowa and be my wife, but I didn't do it because there were other things I had to get done and besides all that I just didn't think that I was anywhere near good enough for you. I still don't but I guess that being way up here and you way down there and I'm using this paper and pen to hide behind like a coward it makes me a little braver to ask you.

If you would be my wife I would come down to Texas to marry up with you and maybe even to stay if you don't want to live up here. It does get awful cold here sometimes.

Well, now that I have said it I am not going to crawfish. I am going to mail this letter to you for sure and suffer the consequences. Please forgive me and don't think less of me if I am being too forward with all this. I will be watching for the mail coach every day until I receive an answer from you. Please do write me an answer even if it is no because I really will be watching that coach.

Now I am not much of a letter writer and I hope that my poor writing won't do anything to influence your decision. If you say yes I will be on the next train to Texas believe me. Please give my kindest regards to your father for me and say hello to little Matt and to my good friend Will Milam if you see him.

Sincerely yours if you will have him,

Bluff Luton

Luton signed the letter, folded it carefully, and sealed it in an envelope. Then he addressed the envelope to Mrs. Emily Fisher, The Cross Timbers Hotel, Henrietta, Texas. He took the letter directly to the post office.

"Good morning, Sarge," said the postal clerk as Luton stepped inside.

"Kirby," said Luton, "how soon will this go out?"

Kirby took the letter from Luton and looked at it.

"Going south," he said.

"Hell, I know that. When will it go?"

"Well, sir, if I get it in the mailbag, it'll go out on tomorrow's stage."

"You see that it does," said Luton.

"Urgent, is it?"

"You just get it into that mailbag," said Luton. "How much?"

* * *

The time dragged slowly by for Bluff Luton the rest of that day. He wondered how he had managed to stay with his job all those years and not go mad. How had he been able to allow himself to sit around Riddle growing soft and lazy? Now his letter was languishing in the post office, waiting for a stagecoach to arrive the next day. He wanted to do something about it, something to make things happen a little faster. Then a moment of panic set in. He tried to imagine Emily's reaction to his letter. Would she laugh? Be insulted? Horrified? What would she think of him? He decided that he had probably accomplished nothing more than making a fool of himself, and he thought about going back to the post office to retrieve his letter.

It was dark outside. He didn't bother looking at his pocket watch, and he had no clock on the wall in his office. He knew, though, that it was plenty late. He had been catching up on paperwork in the office to try to make the time pass more quickly. *Hell, he thought, she ain't going to accept me. She'd be a damn fool to marry me, and she sure ain't a damn fool.* Just the same, he hoped, and because of his hope, he wanted the marshal's office to be in order in case he decided to leave it with little or no notice. And he would leave it, he decided. One way or the other, he would leave it. He would let the letter go. If it made him look the fool, so be it. If Emily would not have him, then he would go somewhere else. The people of Riddle, Iowa, had been good to him, and he didn't want to leave them high and dry, but it was time for him to go. He blew out the flame in the lamp and stepped out onto the board sidewalk. As he was locking the door to the office he thought that he'd go have a drink or two before he turned in for the night. He turned to walk down the sidewalk, and he felt a hard slap between his shoulder blades, just as he also heard the loud, sharp report of a rifle shot. He was aware of that, just as everything went black, and he pitched forward, seeming lifeless, there on the boards in front of his office.

7

Chapter Two

It was hot in Henrietta, Texas. Hal Decker mopped the sweat from his face with a red bandanna as he walked back toward the Cross Timbers Hotel from the post office. He hurried himself along in spite of the heat, knowing that his daughter would be anxious to read the surprise letter from Bluff Luton. Actually, he secretly admitted to himself, he was anxious to find out why, after all this time, Luton had written to Emily. He liked Luton, had liked him from the first time he had met him, really from even before he had met him, for Emily had told him how Luton had protected her and little Matt on the long ride across Missouri and the Indian Territory by rail. Decker had received one letter from Luton not long after Luton had returned to Iowa. It had been brief and polite and had asked Decker to let him know if anyone ever annoyed Emily and Matt again, as he had promised her that she would never be bothered by Fisher again. She had not been, and Decker had not bothered writing to Luton after he had answered that one first letter. All that had taken place nearly eight years ago.

"Grandpa."

Decker glanced up to see Matt Fisher running toward him down the street. Matt was fifteen years old. He was an average size for a boy his age but he had developed a long, lean look. He had green eyes and sandy hair, which, his grandpa thought as he watched him approach, needed cutting just now. A good-looking boy, though, and well behaved. Decker was proud of him.

"Hey, Matt," he said. "You'll never guess what I've got here."

"Looks like the mail to me."

"All right, smart guy," said Decker. "But what's *in* the mail?"

"Letters?"

"Who from? Who have I got a letter from?"

"Well, let's see. The way you're acting, it might be from the president. That's it. You got a letter from Mr. Arthur."

"No, I don't have a letter from Mr. Arthur."

"If you did," said Matt, the mischief building inside him, "you'd probably put it in a frame and hang it up on the wall where everyone could see it. Wouldn't you?"

"No, I wouldn't hang it up on the wall. If I had a letter from chief-muddler Arthur, I'd throw it down in the street right here. Right now. I'd throw it down in the dirt and stamp on it. That's what I'd do. Now, who do I have a letter from?"

"Well, gee, if it's not from Mr. Arthur, I just don't know."

"From Marshal Luton," said Decker.

"From Sarge? Open it up. What's he say?"

"Now just hold on a minute. It's not addressed to me. It's to your mama."

"Well, come on, Grandpa. Hurry up."

"I'm moving as fast as I can. Don't you think that I want to get inside, out of this heat? I'm not as young as you are."

"Were you ever?"

"I was once."

They had reached the front door of the Cross Timbers, and Matt opened the door for Decker. Emily was behind the desk.

"You got yourself a letter here," said Decker, puffing as he stepped into the lobby of his establishment.

"It's from Sarge," shouted Matt. "Read it."

"Well," said Emily, trying to conceal her excitement at the news, "have you told the whole town?"

"No," said Decker, "just Matt."

"Give it to me, then," she said.

Decker handed the letter to Emily, tossed the rest of the mail onto the counter, and found himself a chair. He sat facing his daughter and stared at her.

"Read it," said Matt. "What's he say?"

Emily tore open the envelope and unfolded the letter. She began to read silently to herself.

"Come on, Mom," said Matt. "What's it say?"

"Well," she said, "it's from Bluff."

"We know that," said Decker.

"He says, 'Dear Emily.'"

Emily blushed slightly as she read the greeting. She stiffened her back and continued.

"'Well, I guess that little Matthew is just about growed up by now.'"

"'Little Matthew,'" said Matt, trying to sound disgusted. In spite of his tone of voice, his facial expression betrayed pride in hearing himself mentioned in the first sentence of the letter.

"'It has been a number of years since I have seen you, I know,'" continued Emily, "'and maybe I shouldn't even be writing this letter to you after all this time.'"

"Why shouldn't he?" said Matt.

"Sure he should," said Decker. "Now hush up and listen."

"'I have been in touch with my old friend Will Milam and he has kept me informed about your welfare, as I promised you that no one would bother you anymore, and I want you to know that I have kept my word on that. I did not come back up here to Iowa and just forget about what I had said.'"

Emily paused a moment, wondering what Bluff Luton had done to discourage George Fisher in his pursuit of her and her son. She glanced silently back over the words she had just read.

"Go on," said Matt.

" 'I guess that Will Milam also filled you in on all the details of how things worked out for me on my trip to Texas that time. If you were worrying about me and that Oliver Colfax, as I flattered myself that you might be, I hope that Will told you how all that worked out.

" 'I think that Colfax is one of the strangest ducks I have ever known. He is certainly the most dangerous man I have ever encountered in a lot of years in this funny business that I am in. He could have killed me in Texas, but he chose not to for some reason which no one will ever know probably but just himself.' "

"Colfax could have killed him?" said Matt.

"Milam didn't tell us that part," said Decker.

"No," said Emily, "he didn't."

"What else does it say?" said Matt.

" 'He is a professional killer, I know that, but somehow I can't stop myself from liking the man. If we had met under different circumstances I bet we just might have been pretty good friends.

" 'Well that is not what I am writing this letter to you about, anyway. I am just rambling on trying to get up the courage and find the right words to say what it is that I want to say. Mrs. Fisher . . . Emily. You are certainly—' "

Emily stopped reading out loud. She raced silently through the next paragraph. Her blush now became apparent to her audience.

"Oh," she said.

"What is it?" said Matt.

"Oh, my."

"Mom?"

Emily looked up, first toward Matt, then directly at her father. She was still holding the letter out in front of her as if she were reading it. She spoke softly and with a tone of incredulity.

"This is a proposal," she said. "He wants to marry me."

"Read it," said Matt.

Emily turned and ran to the stairs, then started up them in a hurry.

"No," she said.

Matt started after her.

"Mom."

"Matt," Decker snapped. "Stay here. We'll find out all about it in good time."

Upstairs, Emily went into her room and shut the door. She sat down on the edge of the bed and reread the two pertinent paragraphs. Then, finally, she finished reading the letter. *He wants to marry me*, she thought. *He's proposed. Eight years. Why did he wait eight years? So much time has been lost. So much valuable time. He hasn't even seen me for all that time. Is he sure? I'm eight years older. Matt's eight years older. Still, he did propose. I've got it right here in writing.*

She stood up from the bed and moved to a chair that stood before a small writing desk. She took out a sheet of paper, sat down, prepared inkwell and pen, and thought for a moment, her chin resting on the palm of her left hand, her elbow on the desk. Then suddenly she began to write.

The Cross Timbers
Henrietta, Texas
June 2, 1882

Dearest Bluff,

What a shock to receive a letter from you after all this time, these eight years, and not only that but a proposal of marriage with it. Yes. My answer is yes. Yes, I will marry you and become Mrs. Bluff Luton, and I will go back with you to Iowa, or even to Alaska with you if you wish it. We can also stay in Texas if you say so. We can talk all about that when you get here. Oh, how I wish you had not been afraid to speak eight years ago when you were here. Now we have lost those precious years, and Matt has lost the time when you could have been a father to him as he was growing up. But I will not dwell on the past. We have years yet ahead of us, and I know that they will be wonderful years. Hurry on down to me. I will be waiting anxiously.

Yours,

Emily

Matt and Decker stood up almost together as they saw Emily begin to descend the stairway. She walked slowly, proudly. In one hand she held the envelope and letter from Bluff Luton. In the other she held a sealed envelope. Halfway down the stairs she stopped and held up the letter from Luton.

"As I said before," she announced, "this is a proposal of marriage from Mr. Luton."

"Yeah?" said Decker.

She held up the other hand.

"This is my reply."

"Well?" said Decker.

"What'd you tell him?" said Matt.

Emily walked on down the stairs and over to where the two stood gaping at her. She put an arm around each.

"I said yes. I've accepted his proposal."

Decker put both arms around his daughter and hugged her to him. He kissed her cheek.

"That's great, darling," he said. "I know you'll be happy. I know you will. Sarge is a fine man."

"The finest I know," said Emily, "except for my daddy."

"You going to get married?" said Matt.

"Yes."

"You going to marry Sarge?"

"Yes."

"That means that Sarge'll be my stepdad, don't it?"

"That's right," said Emily.

"Wow. Sarge is famous, Grandpa. Ain't he?"

"Well, he is pretty well-known. At least out here in the west."

"Well, that's all that counts. Mom?"

"What, Matt?"

"What'll I have to call him?"

"You can just go right ahead calling him Sarge if you like. There's nothing wrong with that."

"Yeah. That'll be easy. Mom?"

"Yes?"

"Are you happy?"

"Yes."

"Boy, then I am too. I sure am. Can I read the whole letter now?"

Emily pulled Matt to her and ran a hand through his hair.

"I'll make a deal with you," she said.

"What deal?"

"If you'll take this letter to the post office and see that it gets in the mail, I'll let you read the other one when you get back."

Matt took the letter from Emily's hand and started for the door at a run. On his way out he shouted back over his shoulder to her.

"It's a deal," he said. "Be right back."

As Matt slammed the door behind him, Emily placed her head on her father's chest.

"Oh, Dad," she said, "I'm so happy. I'm very happy. This is what I wanted eight years ago. I'd given up all hope."

"Can I read the letter while Matt's gone?" said Decker.

Chapter Three

Coleman J. Miller stood behind the counter in Miller's Emporium in Riddle. He leaned across the counter, his elbows resting on it, and he was talking in a low voice to two other men. One was Clarence Dry, the local undertaker, the other was Riddle's doctor, Rudolph Gallager. Miller took a breath and was about to say something else when the door of the emporium was thrown open, causing the little bell that dangled in its way to jingle. Miller stopped and straightened himself up. The other two men rolled their bodies around to lounge against the counter in an attempt to appear casual. A shrewd observer would have been immediately suspicious of their behavior.

"Mr. Miller!" shouted the intruder, taking long strides across the room between the shelves of dry goods. "Mr. Miller!"

"What is it, Kirby?" said Miller.

"Mr. Miller, this just came in the mail today," said Kirby, waving a letter in his hand. "What do I do with it?"

"How do I know if you don't show it to me," said Miller, "or at least tell me what it is?"

"Oh, yeah. Well, it's a letter from Texas, and it's addressed to the marshal."

"To Bluff?"

Dry and Gallager exchanged conspiratorial glances.

"Yeah," said Kirby. "Mr. Bluff Luton, it says."

"Let me see it," said Miller.

Kirby handed the letter to Miller, who studied the address for a moment in silence.

"Why are you asking me?" he said. "What's the usual procedure in these circumstances?"

"Well," said Kirby, scratching his head, "I don't know. I never had to deal with these circumstances before. I guess I could look in the book, or write a letter to Washington and ask them, but you're on the Town Council, and this is for Bluff. I thought maybe you'd know what to do with it."

Miller tucked the letter into his inside coat pocket.

"Yeah, you're right, Kirby," he said. "You did the right thing bringing this letter over here. Thanks. I'll take it over to the marshal's office and put it with Bluff's other things and think it over for a bit. Thank you."

"Yeah," said Kirby. "I just, you know, want to do what's right."

"It's fine, Kirby," said Miller. "You'd better get on back to the post office now."

"Yeah. Okay. Well, I'll see you all later."

The three men stood silently watching until Kirby was outside and the door closed behind him. Then they resumed their secretive postures, huddling over the counter. Miller pulled the letter back out of his pocket and looked at it again.

"Mrs. Emily Fisher," he read out loud. "The Cross Timbers Hotel, Henrietta, Texas."

"Wonder what that's all about," said Doc Gallager.

Miller shook his head.

"I don't know, Doc," he said. "I don't have any idea."

Clarence Dry rubbed his long chin with his smooth left hand and puckered his pallid face.

"Hmm," he murmured.

Curly Wade stood on the platform at the railroad depot in Henrietta, Texas. His boss, Will Milam, had sent him into town from the ranch to pick up some freight from the depot. The wagon Curly had driven into town was backed up to the platform. The agent had gone inside. Curly wondered what kind of freight he would have to haul back to the ranch. Will had said that he had no idea what it was.

"I ain't ordered nothing," he had said. "I just got this here message that there was some freight in town at the depot for me. Take the wagon and go after it, but if it's some goddamn wire or something that I didn't order and they want to be paid for it, tell them to go to hell."

The big door was rolled open, and Curly stepped to one side. Then the agent and his assistant came staggering out, one on each end of a long pine box.

"Good Lord A'mighty," said Curly. "What's that?"

"Coffin," said the agent.

The two men struggled to get the box down into the wagon. The agent straightened himself up, standing beside the suddenly ominous freight in the wagon box. He pulled a bandanna out of his pocket and mopped his brow while attempting to catch his breath. He pointed to a piece of paper glued to the top of the box.

"Says here it's from Clarence Dry's Undertaking Establishment in a place called Riddle, Ioway."

"Well, who's in it?" asked Curly.

"Damned if I know. It don't say that."

"It's sent to Will?"

"Will Milam, it says right here. Will Milam, Henrietta, Texas. No mistake."

Curly took off his hat and ran a hand through his hair. He put the hat back on and pulled it down snug.

"Well, I'll be damned," he said.

"Oh," said the agent, "there's a letter came with it for Mr. Milam. Joey, run in and get that letter."

The helper jumped back up on the platform and ran inside. Soon he re-emerged with the letter and handed it to Curly. It was addressed to Will, sure enough, just like the big box, but the return address was different. Curly wrinkled his face in puzzlement. *From Mr. Coleman Miller, Riddle, Ioway. Riddle. Riddle. That's that place where ol' Luton's from, I believe.* He stuffed the letter into a pocket and climbed into the wagon. He figured that he'd find out soon enough. He would probably have to be the one to read the letter to Will.

"Mom, is he coming or ain't he?"

"Isn't he," said Emily Fisher.

"Well, is he?"

Emily looked at her son. He would be grown soon, she thought, but he was still a child in so many ways. He was looking forward, she could tell, to the arrival of Bluff Luton almost as much as she had been—had been because she was about to give up hope. He should have been here by now, she thought. At least she should have heard something more from him. He had said in his letter that if her answer was yes, he would be on the next train. She had answered yes, right away, and he should have been there. She had decided that he wasn't coming. He had thought it over and decided that he didn't want a divorced woman with a half-grown son, after all. She really couldn't blame him any for that. She was just sorry that he had gotten her hopes up in the first place—hers and Matt's. Poor Matt, she thought. He'd never really had a father—not a decent one. At least he had his grandpa. That was something.

"I don't know, Matt," she said. "He should have been here by now."

"Maybe he got busy," said Matt. "He's a marshal. Maybe there was a bank robbery or something and he couldn't come yet."

"Maybe," she said. "Maybe he's not coming at all. Maybe he changed his mind. We have to be ready to face that."

"He wouldn't do that to you, Mom. Not him."

18

There was a knock on the door. Matt looked toward the door, then back at his mother.

"Go ahead and open it," she said.

Matt opened the door, and Decker stepped in. He was holding a copy of *The Police Gazette* in his hand, a place in the pages marked by his index finger. His face wore a solemn look.

"I'm sorry, honey," he said. "I'm so sorry."

"What?" said Emily. "What is it?"

He opened the newspaper and held it out before her. Her eyes found the headline immediately, and it seemed to scream at her inside her brain.

IOWA MARSHAL MURDERED. NO SUSPECTS.

George Fisher sat behind the big desk in his private office. He was studying a contract from which he expected to make a significant amount of money for a modest investment. The door was opened from the outside, and a young man in a three-piece suit stuck his head into the office.

"Mr. Fisher?"

Fisher looked up from his contract.

"What the hell is it, Ryan? I'm busy in here."

Ryan walked on into the big office and tossed the latest copy of *The Police Gazette* onto the desk in front of Fisher. It was opened, and Ryan jabbed a finger at a headline.

"That's him," he said. "Luton. That's the man that was with your wife on the train."

"Are you sure?"

"I'm sure. I recognize him from that picture."

Fisher leaned over the desk and read the story through, then he lounged back in his big chair, his hands folded behind his head. He recalled in an instant how his wife had taken their young son and left him, boarded a train for Texas to go and live with her father. He remembered how he had sent Ryan after them to bring them back to him in Boston.

"What if she won't come back?" Ryan had asked.

"Bring them back," he had said.

Then Ryan had returned alone. He had reported that he had caught up with Emily and Matt on a train somewhere in Missouri but that a yokel had thrown him off the train. Later a man had come to Boston and actually broken into Fisher's home, beaten him, and threatened his life if he ever bothered Emily and Matt again. That had all taken place some eight years earlier. And now that man was dead. That meant that Emily no longer had a protector, a knight in shining armor.

"Ryan," Fisher said, "go get us two tickets to Henrietta, Texas. The next train."

"Two?"

"You heard me. I'm going to take care of this myself."

"Yes, sir," said Ryan, rushing for the door.

Fisher sat alone in his office. He put his feet up on the desk.

"I'll teach that bitch," he said. "I'll show her a thing or two, by God. Nobody runs out on me. Nobody."

Oliver Colfax sat at the hotel bar having a brandy. He wore a white shirt with lace cuffs and collar under a long tail coat with velvet lapels. He appeared to be unarmed. People who knew him or knew his reputation would have doubted that, however. At a table behind him, two men were arguing.

"I say old Slats Potter is the best damned lawman alive," said one.

"Ah," said the other, "you don't know what you're talking about. Potter couldn't walk in Sam Boles's footsteps. Why, I seen Sam one time face down a whole mob. It was damn near the whole town, too. Mean bunch. They had a Chinaman in jail who had raped a white woman. At least that's what they said he had done, and they was dead intent on taking him out and having themselves a lynch party. Sam faced down the whole town and sent them home to bed."

"When was that, Ace? Twenty years ago?"

"Well, no," said the man called Ace. "It wasn't that long ago. Not twenty years."

"It was a while, I bet. I'm saying that right now, today, Slats is the best. Boles may have been good in his day, but he's an old man. The best lawman alive today is Slats Potter."

Colfax turned slightly on his bar stool to face the table. He tossed down his brandy before he spoke.

"Neither one of you gentlemen knows what you're talking about," he said. "I've dealt with both of the men under discussion and found them to be perfectly ordinary. The only really outstanding lawman in the country today is a man named Bluff Luton."

The other two men knew Colfax's reputation. He was a dreaded hired killer, a man who would take on any job for pay and then goad the victim into a fight. It was rumored that for about the past eight years or so Colfax had grown soft in that he was more particular about the assignments he took than he had been in the past. It was said that he feared killing an innocent man. But he was still dangerous.

The man called Ace spoke softly.

"Yeah, I've heard of Luton—somewhere."

The other jumped up out of his seat exultantly.

"By God," he said, "I've got you, then. I've got you. I said alive today."

"What do you mean?" said Colfax.

The man reached down into the seat of a chair next to the one in which he had been sitting and picked up *The Police Gazette.* He fumbled through the pages until he found what he was looking for, then took the paper to Colfax and placed it on the bar before him.

Colfax read the headline, then glanced at the first paragraph to confirm his fear.

"There," said the triumphant debater. "I'm right. It's Slats. No competition."

"Shut up," said Colfax.

"Huh?"

The gloating expression vanished, and the blood seemed to drain from the man's face.

"Mister," said Colfax, "I've never in my life killed a man for pleasure, but if I see you express another hint of joy over the death of this man, I may make an exception of you."

Ace stood up and took the other man by the arm. He tugged gently but insistently.

"Come on," he said. "Let's go somewhere. No offense, Mr. Colfax. It was just bullshit talk. No offense."

The two men left the bar, and Colfax pushed his glass suggestively toward the bartender, who walked over and refilled it.

"That was the finest man I ever knew," said Colfax, not really speaking to the bartender. "The only man I ever met that I would've liked to call my friend."

He looked back down at the newspaper and began to read.

IOWA MARSHAL MURDERED. NO SUSPECTS.

Riddle, Iowa. Town Marshal Bluff Luton, longtime highly respected lawman, was shot to death as he stepped out of his office here on the evening of 19 May. According to Councilman Coleman Miller, there are no suspects in the case. Riddle has been a quiet town during the years Luton was marshal. He was shot in the back with a rifle bullet.

Luton, who was known to his friends as Sarge because of his wartime service, built himself a reputation as a town-taming lawman before settling down some years ago to the Riddle job. He is not known to be survived by any family members.

Colfax sat staring at the newspaper story and running his fingers unconsciously along the ridge of white scar that ran halfway around his neck, a scar that had been put there eight years earlier by Bluff Luton in a fight of Colfax's making. It was ironic, Colfax thought. He had been hired to kill Luton, but he had grown to like the man. He had forced a showdown, anyway, just to prove that he could win, or to give himself the satisfaction of having seen the job through to the end. He wasn't sure. But he had trailed Luton to a mesquite thicket in North Texas, and they had fought. Luton had gotten the drop on him once, but he had slipped in the mud, and then Colfax had jumped him and won. He had aimed his Colt at Luton, then fired into the ground to prove that he could have killed him. Now he was mourning the man's death. He wondered who had killed Luton and why.

A skulking, cowardly bastard, he thought, *to shoot a man in the back with a rifle. A good man, too. Sarge. No suspects, the story says. Hell, I got suspects. What about those so-called range detectives that worked for the Jessups? When Sarge got the Jessups, he spoiled a pretty good setup for those boys. Cost them a pretty penny.*

He tossed down his brandy. Then he stood up and picked up the newspaper from the counter. He folded it and tucked it under an arm. He realized that he had made a decision. He was going to find out who had murdered Sarge, and he was going to kill the son of a bitch.

Chapter Four

Stanley Bragg had bathed and shaved. He liberally splashed his face with lilac water and then greased back his long blond hair. Looking in the mirror, he thought himself to be a handsome young devil. He pulled a bright red shirt on over his head, checked his hair again in the mirror, and resmoothed it just as Victor Bragg stepped into the room.

"You going out, son?" said Victor.

"It's Saturday night, ain't it?"

"Yes. It's Saturday night. Answer my question."

"Yeah, Dad, I'm going out."

Stanley shoved his shirttail into his britches and fastened up his fly.

"Where you going?" said Victor.

"Oh, I don't know. Just out."

"Your mother wants to know where you're going, Stan, and I do, too. I'm asking you."

"I'm not a kid. You don't have to know every move I make, do you? I'm just going out for a good time. It's Saturday night. Don't worry, and, uh, don't wait up, okay?"

Stan reached for his gun belt and wrapped it around his waist.

"Do you have to wear that thing?"

"Wouldn't feel dressed without it."

"The Town Council's passed an ordinance against the wearing of firearms in town."

"Who's going to enforce it?" said Stan. "The marshal's dead."

"Coleman Miller's acting marshal until we can find a replacement."

Stanley laughed as he snugged his low-crowned Plainsman hat down onto his forehead.

"Coleman Miller's a shopkeeper," he said. "He couldn't take a gun away from a schoolgirl."

He hefted the Smith and Wesson .45 at his side with a smirk on his face. Victor could tell that the boy liked the feel of the weapon, liked its weight in his hand or just hanging there at his side.

"Stanley—"

"Oh, hell, don't worry. I ain't going to stay in Riddle, anyhow. There never was no fun to be had in Riddle. I'll probably just ride on across the bridge for a while."

"That's what I figured," said Victor. "Going over to West Riddle. Going out drinking with that no-good Lance Fields."

"You don't know anything about it," said Stan. "You don't even know Lance."

"Stan, a man wearing a gun is just asking for trouble—especially over there. At least leave the gun—please."

"Just leave me alone."

Stan stalked out of the room and brushed past his mother, who was standing in the middle of the living room. She made a feeble gesture toward him as he jerked open the front door.

"Stanley," she said.

The door slammed and he was gone. Victor Bragg walked to his wife and put an arm around her shoulders.

"Victor," she said, "I'm worried about him. What are we going to do about that boy?"

"I don't know, Ruth," said Victor, suddenly sounding old and tired. "I just can't seem to talk to him anymore. He doesn't want to listen to me. He— I don't know."

Leiland Cherry was lying on his back in bed in a rented room in Jack's House, a combination hotel and saloon in West Riddle, Nebraska, formerly known as Blanche's Saloon. There was also a theater attached to the saloon, not much used, and the hotel employed a few women in a lucrative sideline. Cherry, however, was alone. He had removed his shirt and his boots before having stretched himself out on the bed an hour earlier. His hands were folded behind his head, and he stared at the ceiling.

Cherry sat up suddenly on the edge of the bed and arched his back to stretch. He reached for his boots and pulled them on, then stood. He picked up his shirt from where he had left it draped over the back of a straight-backed chair, and pulled it quickly over his head. Soon he was fully dressed, having added necktie, vest, suit coat, and a natty derby. The only things that kept him from looking the part of a successful businessman were the gun belt he had strapped on around his waist holding a Remington Frontier .44 revolver, and the Winchester .44-.40 1873 model rifle he carried in his right hand.

He stepped out into the hallway, not bothering to close the door behind him. He had left the key to the room lying on a table beside the bed. There was no luggage, nothing of his left behind in the room. He walked down the hallway to the back door, opened it, stepped out onto the landing, and started down the stairs to the alley below.

Dolf Hogner had his wagon loaded and was ready to go back home to the farm. He sat on the wagon seat impatiently smoking his pipe. Hogner didn't like town, so he was relieved when the door to the dry goods store opened and he saw Mary Ellen step out onto the sidewalk. They'd be out of town soon, and headed for home. A few years back, Hogner wouldn't ever have stopped in West Riddle for his supplies. Even though it was a little farther, he'd have driven across the bridge to Riddle, but since Marshal Blue Steele had settled in West Riddle, the town had become a little more civilized.

Inside Jack's House, at a table by the big window in front, Stan Bragg and Lance Fields sat, a bottle of whiskey between them. The evening was yet young, but they were already feeling good. As Mary Ellen Hogner stepped down into the street to move toward her father's wagon, Fields saw her through the window. He tossed down his drink, shoved his chair back from the table, and stood up.

"Be right back," he said.

"Where you going?" asked Stan.

"Stay here. Watch the bottle."

Fields ran out into the street to intercept Mary Ellen. He stepped directly into her path and swept off his hat in a courtly gesture comically out of keeping with his general appearance and surroundings.

"Good evening, Miss Hogner," he said.

"Good evening, Mr. Fields," said Mary Ellen. She attempted to step around Fields, but he adroitly sidestepped to get himself back into her path.

"I have to be on my way, Mr. Fields," she said.

"I thought you might like to come into Jack's House to have a little drink with me. I'd be pleased if you would."

"No thank you. My father's waiting for me."

Fields glanced over his shoulder and saw Hogner waiting in the wagon. The old man was looking right at him. Fields turned back to Mary Ellen.

"Oh, well," he said, "you could just tell him to run on along, and I can bring you home safe a little later."

"He would never agree to that if I asked him," said Mary Ellen. "And what's more, I would never ask it."

"Why not? You scared of him?"

"I don't want to stay in town with you. I don't want to go into a saloon. I don't want to have a drink with you or with anyone else. I don't drink. Please get out of my way."

She made another attempt to step around him, but Fields grabbed her by the arm.

"Mary Ellen—"

Dolf Hogner came down from his wagon seat as quickly as he could manage it and headed for Fields, but he had just begun the trip when a long-haired young man wearing a town marshal's badge stepped into the street and took hold of Fields by the nape of the neck. Fields automatically slapped at the six-gun hanging at his side, but the lawman grabbed his right wrist before he could pull out the weapon.

"Settle down, Lance."

"Damn," said Fields.

"Thank you, Mr. Steele," said Mary Ellen. She hurried on to meet her father. Hogner put an arm around his daughter. As he moved with her back to the wagon, he snarled at Fields over his shoulder.

"No good."

"Good night, Mr. Hogner—Mary Ellen," said Steele. He still had a hand on Fields's neck. "Lance, you go on back inside and get drunk and stay out of trouble. Leave folks alone."

"Hell, Blue," said Fields, "I just invited the lady for a drink. Okay? I ain't looking for trouble. Plenty gals inside, anyhow."

"All right. Go on back in, then."

Steele stood in the street and watched Fields go back into Jack's House. Then he turned and walked away. Inside the saloon, Fields sat back down and grabbed for the bottle, pouring himself a fresh drink. He downed it in a gulp and poured another.

"That damned half-breed," he said.

"Who?" said Stan. "The marshal? Steele?"

"Mr. Half-breed Marshal Bluford Steele," said Fields. "The son of a bitch. He's going to go too goddamned far one time."

"Forget him, Lance. Hell, don't let him spoil the night for us. Probably be a game in here in a little while, you reckon?"

Fields laughed.

"Yeah. Always is. I ain't worried about that damn Indian. Hell, I forgot him already. Son of a bitch."

He poured himself another drink.

"What was he bothering you for, anyway?" said Stan. "He got it in for you or something?"

"Stuck-up bitch," said Fields.

"What?"

"Mary Ellen. She's got her nose so far up in the air, she might get drowned if it rains. Damn Indian thought he was protecting a white woman's reputation. Shit."

"Lance, how'd this town get itself stuck with a Indian for a lawman, anyway?"

Lance Fields poured himself another drink.

"I don't remember it very good," he said. "I was just a kid. Eight or ten years ago. I don't know. Anyhow, they say this was a pretty tough town in those days. Steele come along and cleaned it out. They'd killed a friend of his or something. They made him town marshal. That's about it."

"It ain't right," said Stan.

"To hell with him. Hey, Jack. We need another bottle here."

Jack came out from behind the bar and brought a bottle to the table.

"Where's the girls?" said Fields.

"They'll be down in about twenty minutes or so," said Jack, glancing at the watch from his vest pocket. "You boys got yourselves an early start tonight. They'll be here in a little bit."

Down the street in the marshal's office, Blue Steele poured himself a cup of coffee and sat down with it at his desk. He would have to check things out back at Jack's House in a little while, he knew. Fields was potential trouble—always. A spoiled kid who had grown up in West Riddle, he had been on the edge of trouble for years. Sooner or later he'd get himself right into the middle of it. And now he had this banker's kid, this Bragg from across the river, with him. Steele didn't know Bragg well, but he seemed like a suitable companion for Fields.

Steele sipped his coffee. He resented the intrusion into his thoughts of Fields and Bragg—wished they'd stayed out of town on this particular night. He wanted to concentrate on the problem of figuring out who had shot Luton. It wasn't his job. It was outside his jurisdiction, across the state line. But Luton was his friend, and Coleman Miller wouldn't be able to figure it out. Even if he could figure it out, he wouldn't be able to do anything about it. Miller was a businessman and a small-town politician. He wasn't a lawman. Besides that, in spite of the fact that the two towns were in separate states, they were only divided from each other by the river, and their main streets were actually connected to each other by the bridge. A murder in Riddle was a threat too close to home for comfort.

It was late when Steele decided to walk back down to Jack's House. He found the place no more rowdy than usual for a Saturday night. According to Jack, Fields and Bragg had staggered out of the place just a few minutes earlier.

Chapter Five

Oliver Colfax eased himself down out of the saddle. He was sore and stiff from the long ride. He wrapped the reins loosely around the hitch rail and rubbed the pinto's neck. She was a good horse, but he would much have preferred an easier ride. The railroad hadn't reached Riddle, so the choices were two: stage or horseback. Colfax had decided that the horseback ride was preferable to the constant battering his body would have received on the stage. He glanced up and down the near deserted main street of the town. Sunday morning, he thought, and the farmers are all in church. He needed a stable for the pinto and a meal for himself. A drink would set right, too, after the long ride. Then a hotel room so he could settle in temporarily, and he would be ready to get to work. There were people to meet and questions to ask so he could get on the trail of Luton's killer—or killers.

Victor Bragg was not in church that morning. He and Ruth had gotten themselves ready to go to service as usual, but just as they were ready to leave the house, Ruth had taken a look into Stan's room. He wasn't there. The bed had not been slept in. Victor had hurried out to the barn where he had discovered that Stan's horse was not at home, either. He had told Ruth not to worry, that Stan was getting wilder all the time and he had most likely just decided not to come home that night. Probably he had been out late drinking with that Fields boy and had stayed over with him rather than ride home late at night, alone and drunk. But even as he told his wife not to worry, he worried himself.

Victor Bragg saddled himself a horse. Telling Ruth once again not to worry, he left her at home and rode off on horseback in search of his errant son. Riding down the main street of Riddle, Bragg noticed the trail-worn stranger with the pinto, but he was much too concerned with the welfare of his son to give him much thought. He rode onto the bridge and crossed into the neighboring Nebraska town. He wondered if he would find the marshal in his office on a Sunday morning, or if he would have to go to his home and roust him out. In his mind he rehearsed his opening line. "Marshal, my son didn't come home last night. I'm sure he was here." But before he could get any farther along with his lines, he came in view of the marshal's office. Before it, tied to the hitch rail, was Stan's horse. Bragg hastened his mount to the rail, swung down out of the saddle, quickly slung the reins around the rail, and raced into the office. Blue Steele sat behind his desk. Stan Bragg was pacing the floor. The youngster stopped abruptly as his father burst into the room. Victor Bragg hesitated a moment, taking in the situation, then he closed the door behind him.

"Dad," said Stan, "what are you doing here?"

"You didn't come home last night. Your mother's worried sick. I came looking for you. That is, I came looking for the marshal to ask him to help me find you. I didn't expect you to be here."

Bragg turned to face Steele.

"I'm Victor Bragg," he said. "This is my son."

Steele stood up behind his desk and held out his hand. Bragg hesitated, then shook it dutifully and perfunctorily.

"I'm Bluford Steele," said the marshal.

"I know," said Bragg. "I came looking for you. What's going on here? Is Stanley under arrest?"

"No," said Steele. "Nothing like that. Stan came to my house early this morning and woke me up. Why don't you have a seat here and let me get you a cup of coffee?"

Bragg thought for an instant of saying indignantly that he hadn't come across the river for a friendly chat and a cup of coffee, but he sensed that the coffee probably had been offered as a prelude to a long explanation. He shrugged off his initial belligerence, at least for the time being, and sat down in a captain's chair that stood beside Steele's desk. Steele went to the coffeepot on the stove in the far corner of the room. He poured Bragg a cup and handed it to him, then refilled his own and Stanley's cups. Finally he sat back down behind his desk.

"Well?" said Bragg.

Stanley had turned his back on his father and stood facing the wall.

"Stan," said Steele, "come on over here and sit down."

Stanley obeyed the marshal, taking a chair on the opposite side of the desk from his father.

"Now," said Steele, "start all over and tell me the whole story from beginning to end. That way your father will get to hear it all from you, and I get to hear it a second time. See if I missed anything the first time through. You might even remember something you left out the first time. Okay? Go on."

Stanley glanced at his father and looked quickly back at the marshal. He sipped at his coffee.

"You got a smoke, marshal?" he said. "I must have lost mine."

Steele took a sack and some papers out of his desk drawer and tossed them across the desk to Stanley. The young man nervously rolled himself a smoke. Steele tossed him a match, which Stan scratched on the side of the desk. He lit the cigarette, took a deep draw, and exhaled slowly.

"Thanks," he said. "Well, like I told you before, I come over here last night, it was maybe six o'clock, and I met Lance over at Jack's House. We had a few drinks, Lance more than me. We was sitting at a table right up by the front window, you know, and Lance saw this girl walking along in the street. He told me to wait, and he went outside to talk to her. I didn't know her, but when Lance came back later, he said that her name was Mary Ellen. 'Course, I couldn't hear what they were saying, but Lance was trying to talk to her, trying to get her to come into Jack's for a drink, I think, and she looked like she was just trying to get away from him. Her old man, he was waiting in the wagon, he looked like he was coming after her—or after Lance. I don't know. But that's just when you come along and got ahold of Lance. Then Mary Ellen and the old man left, and Lance come back to the table with me. You left, too."

Stanley stopped to sip his coffee and take another deep drag on the cigarette. Victor Bragg shifted his weight nervously in the captain's chair.

"Well, Lance was mad when he sat back down with me," said Stan. "I could tell. He drank faster, and he cussed you some. Said one time you'd go too far. Said he hadn't done nothing wrong, and really, Marshal, I couldn't see as how he had. Anyhow, he cussed Mary Ellen some, too. Said she was a stuck-up bitch.

"Pretty soon the girls came down, and then some guys came in and a poker game got started. We played cards awhile, but Lance was losing, so we quit. I guess we were both a little drunk, and I don't know how late it was, but Lance got to talking about Mary Ellen again, only this time he didn't cuss her and didn't call her stuck-up. He said that he bet that she was just scared of her old man. He bet that she really did want to come on inside with him. He said we ought to ride on out to her place to see her. He said—"

Stanley glanced at his father for the first time since he had started talking. Victor Bragg was staring intently at him. Stan looked away, ducked his head, and took a last drag on his cigarette. He snuffed the butt on the floor.

"Go on, Stan," said Steele. "What else did Lance say?"

"He said that after he was done, I could have her, too. I know it sounds crazy. I wouldn't have gone with him if I hadn't been drunk."

"God," said Victor Bragg.

Blue Steele held up a hand to silence Bragg.

"Go on, Stan," he said.

"Well, we mounted up and headed out for her house. I didn't know where it was—still don't, 'cause we never got there. We headed south. I remember that. We took one of these side streets, and it went out of town south, kind of alongside the river. There's big trees on both sides of the road. We was singing and laughing and having a big time. The last thing I remember Lance saying was he said, 'We're almost there now, boy.'

"Then there was a shot. Rifle shot, I could tell. God, it was loud. It spooked my horse and I fell off. It kind of knocked the wind out of me, I guess. I remember I wondered if I'd been shot. I just laid there. I don't know how long. Pretty soon I knew that I wasn't shot, and my breath come back. My head still wasn't clear though. It was quiet—real quiet and dark. I said Lance's name, but he didn't answer me. Then I rolled over and got up on my hands and knees and couldn't see our horses—neither one of them. I crawled along a ways, saying Lance's name over and over, and then I found him. I just crawled up on him. He was laying there shot dead.

"I crawled off the road and hid and pulled out my gun, but there wasn't nobody around. After a while I eased on out of there and looked around for my horse—or his—but I never found them. Finally I just started walking back. I guess I walked all night nearly. I was almost back to town when I come across my horse. The damn thing was just standing there in the road. I come straight to your house, Marshal."

Colfax had checked into a hotel room, boarded the pinto, had a meal and a glass of brandy, and asked directions to the town marshal's office. The office was locked up, he had been told. It had been since the marshal had been killed. For the time being, Mr. Coleman Miller, the mayor, was acting as town marshal. He could usually be found at Miller's Emporium on Main Street, but not, of course, on a Sunday. He'd be at church until noon. Then he'd likely go home. Colfax found the church and waited outside. It was twelve-fifteen by the Illinois watch Colfax carried before the big front doors of the church were opened and the preacher stepped out to impose his handshake on everyone who tried to pass him by. Colfax moved to the bottom of the stairs. The first man to escape the preacher was captured by the professional assassin.

"Excuse me," said Colfax.

"Yes?"

"I'm looking for Mr. Coleman Miller. Is he in the church?"

"Why, uh, yes. He was in church this morning. Always is. He'll be coming out soon."

"Would you mind just waiting here long enough to point him out to me? I've never met the man."

The churchgoer's eyes wandered down to the Colt strapped high on Colfax's waist and pushed slightly around to the front.

"You got business with Mr. Miller, have you?"

"That's why I'm here," said Colfax.

"Well, uh, sure. I guess it's all right. Why, here he comes now. Mr. Miller. Mr. Miller, this gentleman is looking for you."

Having done his duty, the man hurried off. Miller walked down the stairs and stepped up to Colfax.

"I'm Coleman Miller," he said.

"My name is Oliver Colfax."

"What can I do for you, Mr. Colfax?"

"Is there someplace private we can go to talk?"

Miller thought he could invite Colfax to his house, or they could use his private office in the back of the store, but he wasn't sure that he liked the man's looks. His revolver, in its strange position that seemed peculiarly calculated to draw one's gaze, was especially bothersome to Miller. Then there was the name. Miller was certain that he had heard it before.

"The café down the street," he said. "We can find a quiet table there."

"All right."

"Can I have another cup of coffee?" said Stan Bragg. His head was hurting and he was groggy. He had drunk entirely too much whiskey the night before, had suffered a terrible fright, seen his friend dead, walked most of the night, and had not slept.

"Sure," said Steele, "help yourself."

Victor Bragg had dozens of things he wanted to say to his son, but he decided that his best immediate course was silence and patience. Stan went to the stove and poured himself a refill. Then he went back to his chair.

"Stan," said Steele, "do you know of anyone who'd want to kill Lance?"

"No," said Stan. "I don't know. Maybe Mary Ellen's old man, but he didn't know we were coming out there."

"No one else? What about the cardplayers last night?"

"Hell, Lance was losing. They didn't have no reason to be mad at him."

"Did he get mad over losing?"

"No, he was laughing about it."

"How were you doing?"

"What?"

"Were you losing, too?"

"I won a little and then lost it. I broke even, pretty much."

"So you don't think that anyone from the card game was mad enough to have shot Lance?"

"No. I don't think so."

"Did Lance have any trouble with anyone in town last night?"

"No," said Stan. He thought a moment, then added, "Only you."

It would have been convenient had Fields had some trouble in town, Steele thought, because then whoever he had argued with, fought with, whatever, easily could have followed him out of town. But Stan's story was confirmed by what Jack had told Steele right after the two had ridden out of town. There had been no trouble, Jack had said. Of course, someone in town could have had a reason to kill Lance and not have made his feelings obvious. It still could have been someone from town who followed the two young men and shot Lance.

"Mr. Bragg," said Steele, "why don't you go ahead and take Stan home? I know he needs some rest. I've got to go out and find that body. I'll have some more questions for you, Stan. I'll come over to see you later."

Colfax had already had a brandy, and it was still early in the day. Back at the café with Miller, he ordered coffee. Miller did the same. With their coffee on the table and the waiter gone away to a safe distance, Miller decided again to get right down to business.

"Now," he said, "what can I do for you, Mr. Colfax?"

"Bluff Luton was a friend of mine," said Colfax. "I want to know who killed him."

Miller put down his cup and looked into the other's eyes, but whatever it was he was looking for, he did not find it.

"I don't know who killed him, Mr. Colfax."

"Nevertheless, you know more than I do. I want you to tell me what you know."

Chapter Six

Colfax hadn't learned much from Miller. Luton had been shot in the back late one evening as he stepped out of his office. The shot might have come from the river bridge. The weapon used was probably a .44-40 rifle. There were no suspects. For a man who had been a law officer most of his life, Luton surprisingly had no known enemies. Riddle had been a quiet town. Miller had suggested that the man they sought must be someone from Luton's past.

"What about West Riddle?" Colfax had asked.

"Sarge stayed away from there," Miller had answered. "Outside of his jurisdiction."

Based on the information he had gleaned from Miller, Colfax decided that the killer must be someone from the trip to Texas Luton had made eight years earlier. Apparently Luton hadn't told anyone in Riddle any of the details of that trip, but Colfax knew that Luton had gone down there deliberately to kill two men. The Jessups had murdered his younger brother years earlier and had disappeared. Luton had heard that they were back in the vicinity of Wichita Falls and had gone to kill them. As it turned out, the Jessups themselves had been the ones who had sent the word. They had wanted to get him first. So, on his trip to Texas, Luton had been the target of a number of hired killers. Colfax knew all this because he had been one of them. But Colfax in those days had been a professional killer with a peculiarity. He had ascribed to the philosophy of the depravity of man, and he therefore believed that any given man deserved to die. Yet with each new job, Colfax felt the need to reestablish the validity of his philosophy, so he would wait until he had found enough evidence of his intended victim's meanness to satisfy himself once again. Only then would he finish his assignment.

Bluff Luton had been a problem. The more Colfax saw of Luton, the more he found to like—to admire, even—and so for the first time he had not finished a job. He had tracked Luton down, fought with him, and won. He had proved to himself and to Luton that he could have done it had he wanted to. Then he had left. He had left Luton behind, defeated but alive, and with him he had left his profession. Luton had challenged Colfax's philosophy, the foundation of his profession, and it had been found wanting.

In the meantime, however, Luton and his Texas friends, Will Milam and Curly Wade, had killed the Jessups and several of their other hired killers, so Colfax figured that Texas would be the place to look for Luton's killer. Only there, it seemed, had Luton made enemies in recent years. Besides that, Miller had told Colfax that Luton's body had been shipped back to Texas to Will Milam for burial. That was probably as it should be, Colfax thought. At any rate, he would go to Texas, and while he was there, he would visit the grave.

No sooner had Colfax left Riddle than the mayor sent for Clarence Dry and Rudy Gallager. Impatiently he paced the floor behind the counter in the emporium, and when the small bell hanging above his front door sounded to indicate someone's entrance, he whirled anxiously, only to see Mrs. Mauldin come briskly into the store. She fondled material from several different bolts of cloth before making a decision, and when Dry came into the store, Miller was busy wrapping Mrs. Mauldin's purchase. As she opened the door to leave, Gallager showed up. The three men huddled together at the counter cautiously, even though there was not another soul in the building.

"We may have a problem," said Miller.

Blue Steele decided to cross the bridge to see the mayor and acting town marshal of Riddle. He had already ridden out to the scene of the killing of Lance Fields and had recovered the body and Fields's horse. He had paid a visit to the Hogners and learned nothing except that they had heard a single rifle shot in the night. It must have been the shot that killed Fields. They had seen neither Fields, nor young Bragg, after having left town that night. Steele did not tell the Hogners what Stan Bragg had revealed to him of his and Fields's plan—the reason they had ridden out that particular road where Fields had met with his demise.

Steele was going to Riddle because Lance Fields had been shot in the back. It appeared to Steele to have been a calculated murder. From the looks of the wound on the body, he guessed that the weapon used had been a .44-40. *There's a connection,* he told himself, *or else it's a hell of a coincidence, and I don't believe in coincidence.*

When Steele stepped into Miller's Emporium, Dry and Gallager each moved slightly aside to break up their huddle at the counter with Miller. Dry continued to rest his elbows on the counter, glancing over his shoulder to see who was coming. Gallager turned clear around to face Steele, and leaned back casually against the counter.

"Steele," said Miller, "we haven't seen you over here for a while. What can I do for you?"

"Did you hear about Lance Fields?" said Steele.

"Young fellow that was killed last night over on your side? Out with Vic Bragg's boy?"

"That's the one."

"Well, that's all we've heard. Just what I told you."

"Mr. Miller," said Steele, "you said that Marshal Luton was shot in the back from a distance with a .44-40 slug."

"We don't know for sure that it was a .44-40," said Gallager. "That's an educated guess."

"Okay," said Steele. "Well, Lance Fields was shot in the back last night—from a distance by someone with a rifle. It looks to me like it was a .44-40."

"You think the two incidents are related?" asked Doc Gallager.

"They sure are a lot alike," said Steele.

"And coming so close together when there hasn't been anything like this happen around here for years," said Miller. "Even on your side, since you've been there—what is it? Eight years now? You haven't had a killing, have you?"

"Not until last night."

"It sure sounds like the same man did them both," said Dry.

"But who?" said the doc.

"I don't know," said Steele, "but we do have a little more to go on now."

"What's that?" asked Miller.

"Now we can look for someone who had some reason to kill both Luton and Fields."

"I don't know of any connection between the two," said Miller, "and I can't imagine one."

"Well, in keeping with our jurisdictions," said Steele, "I suggest that you continue to concentrate on the Luton case while I follow up on this Fields killing, but I think that we ought to get our heads together pretty regular—especially whenever we come up with anything new."

"Agreed," said Miller.

"Right now, with your permission, since he lives over here, I'd like to go have another talk with Stanley Bragg."

"Sure," said Miller. "Go right ahead."

Steele turned to leave the store, and Clarence Dry hurriedly whispered into Miller's ear.

"Oh, yeah," said Miller. "Steele, wait."

Steele turned back around.

"Yeah?"

"You ever heard of a Colfax? Oliver Colfax?"

"A professional killer," said Steele.

"He was just here asking questions about Sarge. He said he's looking for Sarge's killer."

George Fisher spent most of his train time in the dining car. It was the only way he could figure to insulate himself from the common riffraff out in the passenger cars. Between his meals, he drank. He was ill-tempered, and Ryan found every opportunity he could to leave his boss alone with his drinks. He was afraid to stay gone for too long at a time, though. He knew that would aggravate Fisher even more.

Ryan had just decided that he'd better go back into the dining car to re-join Fisher. As he approached the table and pulled out a chair, Fisher tossed down a drink and scowled up at him.

"Where the hell have you been?" he said.

Ryan didn't have to try to answer, for Fisher yelled at the waiter to bring him another drink. Ryan decided that he could afford to have another, and made a motion to the waiter.

"You got your gun?" said Fisher.

Ryan patted his chest on the left side.

"Right here," he said. He wondered how many more times his boss would ask him that same question.

"Where the hell are we, anyway?" said Fisher.

"Somewhere in Missouri, Mr. Fisher," said Ryan. "I think."

"Goddamn."

Fisher leaned across the table toward Ryan, as if he would impart some highly confidential information.

"People who live out here are no better than wild animals, are they, Ryan?" he said. "Savages. White, black, or red. If they live out here, they're goddamned savages."

"Yes, sir," said Ryan.

The waiter set the drinks on the table, and each man paid for his own. Fisher watched the waiter walk away, then turned back to his captive.

"Ryan," he said, "why would a woman take her own kid out of Boston and come out to damn wilderness? Can you tell me that? Why?"

"I don't know, sir."

"There's no reason. That's why. You know what the problem was?"

"No, sir."

"I was too soft. Too easy on her. I should have slapped the shit out of her at least once a day. That's what they want out of a man. All of them. Believe me. Are you married, Ryan?"

"No, sir. I'm not."

"Well, take it from me. Don't get married. Don't ever get married. But if you do, remember: Slap the shit out of her once a day and she'll come crawling to you. Make sure she knows who wears the pants. A man's home is his goddamned castle, Ryan. We've got to keep it that way."

"Yes, sir."

"When I get my hands on that slut, I'll show her what a real man's like. I'll show her. Take my kid away from me. Shit."

"Stan, is there anything else you can think of to tell me?"

"No, Marshal," said Stanley Bragg. "I told you everything already."

"The last time we talked, you hadn't had any sleep. You had been out walking most of the night just after your friend got killed right beside you. Not only that, you were drunk—or hung over."

"Well, I can't think of a damn thing I haven't already told you."

Steele rocked back in the chair in which he sat on the front porch of the Bragg home until he was leaning against the front wall of the house, the chair perched on its two back legs.

"You never got to Hogner's place?"

"No, we never."

"You didn't see anyone on the road?"

"It was dark as hell. We didn't see no one."

"Did you hear anything?"

"Just the shot. We was making too damn much noise our own selves. Laughing and singing and such. You know. We were . . . pretty drunk."

"Did you and Lance get into any arguments that evening— about anything?"

"No. We never— What the hell are you trying to do? You think I shot him?"

"I don't think anything, Stanley. I'm just asking questions. Okay, forget about the events of that particular evening. Can you think of anyone at all who might've been holding a grudge on Lance—for any reason?"

"Well, I—"

"Think hard, Stanley."

"Hell, I don't even have to talk to you. You're not the lawman over here. Not in this state, you ain't."

"No," said Steele, "but I got the cooperation of your mayor and acting marshal before I came over here to see you. It's legal and it's official. Stanley, was Lance Fields a friend of yours?"

"Sure he was. You know that."

"Well, all I'm trying to do is get information that will help me find out who killed him. That's all. Don't you want to see the killer punished?"

"Yeah. Yeah, sure, but I can't think of anything to help. Nothing."

"There's another possibility, Stan."

"What?"

"You said it was awful dark out there."

"That's right."

"Could the killer have shot the wrong man?"

Chapter Seven

"Hello, Hal."

Startled, Hal Decker looked up from behind the counter in the lobby of the Cross Timbers Hotel. He recognized George Fisher immediately. The other man, the short, tough-looking one, he had never seen before.

"George," he said, "what are you doing here?"

"This is an employee of mine, Hal. Mr. Ryan. Ryan, this gentleman is my father-in-law, Mr. Hal Decker. He owns this . . . establishment."

Ryan nodded.

"What do you want, George?" said Decker.

"I came to get my wife and kid."

"You've no claim on Emily—nor on Matt. The divorce decree gave Emily exclusive custody of Matt. It's been more than eight years, George. Matt don't even know you. You wouldn't know him if he was to walk right up to you. It's over, George. Forget it."

"I've got four tickets to Boston on the train leaving here day after tomorrow. They'll be with me."

"Get out of here, George. Leave it alone."

Fisher walked up close to the counter with Ryan in step, to his left and one pace behind.

"I want to see them," he said. "Where are they?"

Decker set his jaw and glared defiantly at Fisher.

"That's all right," said Fisher. "There's plenty of time. I'll get them. Right now just give us a room."

"There's another hotel just down the street," said Decker.

Ryan looked questioningly at Fisher, who glanced casually away and shrugged his shoulders. Suddenly Ryan's left hand shot out, grabbing Decker by the shirtfront and dragging him halfway across the counter. With his right, Ryan slapped Decker viciously across the face three times.

"He said get us a room."

"Go to hell," said Decker.

Ryan's right hand grabbed a handful of Decker's hair and smashed his face down onto the counter. Then Ryan held Decker's head up by the hair in preparation for a crashing blow to the jaw.

"Grandpa."

Ryan hesitated. Fisher looked around. Matt was standing on the landing halfway up the stairs.

"Matt?" said Fisher.

"Who are you? What are you doing here?"

"Let him go," Fisher said over his shoulder to Ryan. Then he looked back at the boy on the landing. "Yeah," he said, "you're Matt."

"You get out of here," said Matt. "I'm going to get the sheriff."

He started on down the stairs.

"Never mind, Matt," said Decker. "They're leaving anyway."

"Yeah," said Fisher. "That's right. Just down the street, you say? Let's go, Ryan. Matt, we'll be seeing you. Oh, yeah, and, uh, tell your mother I'll be seeing her, too."

*　*　*

Colfax had arrived in Henrietta on the same train as had Fisher
and Ryan, but he had not seen them. He might have recognized
Ryan had he come across him, but he had never seen Fisher and
so wouldn't have known him, anyway. He had not bothered to
stop at the hotel to see Hal Decker and Emily Fisher. He knew
who Decker was but did not feel that he really knew the man, and
he had no way of knowing that Emily Fisher and Bluff Luton had
been in touch with each other. As far as Colfax knew, Luton had
ridden away from Texas eight years ago and never looked back.
Colfax had come to Texas to see Will Milam. He had gone
straight to a stable after getting off the train to rent a horse, and
he rode right out to the Milam ranch. Seeing a rider approaching
from a distance, Will Milam stood on his front porch waiting.
When Colfax stopped the horse in front of the porch, Milam was
the first to speak.

"It's Colfax, ain't it?" he said.

"That's right."

"It's been a long time."

"Yeah."

"Well, climb on down and come in the house. One of the
boys'll take care of your horse."

Inside, Colfax found himself sinking into a large, overstuffed,
leather-covered chair, a cup of black coffee on the table to his
right. Milam sat in a similar easy chair directly facing him. He
had a glass of whiskey.

"Now, Mr. Colfax," said Milam, "what is it that brings you
back here?"

"I'm looking for the man that killed Sarge Luton."

"That happened up in Ioway," said Milam. "Nobody down
here don't know nothing about that. Bluff hadn't been around
here since that time you was here. You know. Eight years, I
think. Something like that."

There was something about Milam, about his voice or his
eyes—something Colfax couldn't pin down or put a name to, but
it made him suspicious.

48

"I've been up to Iowa, Milam," he said. "Nobody up there seems to have any ideas about this thing. Riddle is a quiet, peaceful little town. Sarge made it that way years ago. Those people don't seem to think he had an enemy in the world."

"He must have had one," said Milam.

Colfax sipped his coffee.

"He was killed by a professional," he said. "A hired killer."

"How do you know that?"

"Long rifle shot in the back just as he stepped out of his office. It sounds like a professional job to me. The man who hired the killer could be anyone anywhere. I'm thinking about those men the Jessups had hired on here to protect this place for them. The ones that Sarge ran off."

"That was eight years ago, man."

"There's no one else."

Milam pushed himself up out of his chair and paced the floor.

"Colfax," he said, "we didn't hardly run them ol' boys off. Me and Curly and Bluff, we come out here to fight, all right—to get this place back from them that stole it from me. Bluff had his own personal reasons, too. You know they had killed his brother. There was just the two Jessups and three gunmen left out here. We stopped just up on that rise out there. We was trying to figure out our next move when we heard some shots from the house. Them three come out right after that. Said they was leaving. Said they didn't want to fight us for the Jessups. We let them go."

"The shots?" said Colfax.

"We come on down here and found both Jessups dead. Them three had killed them."

Colfax sat quiet for a moment, stroking his chin. He took another sip of coffee.

"I never knew that," he said. "I always figured that you and Sarge had got them."

"No. We never."

"Damn," said Colfax. He stood up and walked across the room opposite from where Milam stood, then turned to face Milam again.

"It could still be them," he said. "They rode out because of him. He cost them a considerable sum of money, and he hurt their professional pride."

"That's a funny way to refer to it," said Milam.

"It may seem like it to you, but I know what I'm talking about."

Milam tossed down what whiskey remained in his glass. He stiffened as he faced Colfax directly.

"There is someone else," he said.

"Who?"

"You, Colfax. You were one of them. And you followed him out of here when he left. You didn't get him that time. Maybe you got him this time. It could be you."

"There's nothing wrong with your reasoning," said Colfax. "If I was in your place, I'd have the same thought. But I didn't do it. I wasn't one of them, either. I was hired separate. I always work alone. I was hired to kill him, and I intended to kill him. I told him so. But I grew to like him, and I've never shot a man in the back. And you're wrong about one other thing."

"Oh, yeah?"

"When I followed him out of here, I did get him. I finished my job. I didn't kill him, but I could have, and he knew it, so I figured my job was done and I had won. The Jessups were dead, anyhow. No one was left to pay me."

"That's your story," said Milam, "but how do I know it's true?"

"You don't," said Colfax with a sigh, "but if I had killed him, why would I be poking around here now?"

"I don't know. You tricked me once, though. It was me who told you where he was headed when he left here. You followed him."

"Look," said Colfax, "you don't have to believe me. I don't give a damn. You don't have to trust me. I just want two things from you and I'll be on my way. Have you heard anything about those three gunslingers lately?"

"The three that we let ride off?"

"That's who I'm talking about."

Milam looked at Colfax for a long moment, then he shrugged his heavy shoulders.

"The one they called Rat-face," he said, "he got himself killed, I heard, down in Waco. Couple of years ago."

"And the other two?"

"Simpson and Bradley? I heard they was operating up in the Nations. I don't know just what they're up to up there. That's the last I heard."

"Which one?"

"Choctaw, I think. You said two things."

"I want to see Sarge's grave."

Chapter Eight

Colfax rode slowly back to Henrietta. Something didn't set right. He was bothered by Milam's seeming nervousness and hesitancy. Eight years ago Colfax had questioned the rancher about Luton, and he had gotten all the answers he had wanted. He couldn't figure out why Milam was so different with him this time. Eight years ago there had been at least the possibility that Colfax would try to kill Luton, yet Milam had talked to him. This time, with Luton already dead, why was Milam so edgy?

He had taken Colfax out back of the ranch house to the middle of a wide-open stretch of prairie and pointed out a fresh mound of dirt.

"Right here," he had said.

"No marker?" Colfax had said.

"Didn't seem necessary," Milam had replied.

Something was wrong somewhere. Colfax couldn't pin it down, but it bothered him. In the first place, why hadn't that Miller up there in Iowa just buried Luton there? Why send the body all the way down to Henrietta, Texas, to a man Luton hadn't seen in eight years—and before that in twenty? Maybe Luton and Milam had been close friends once, but they sure hadn't remained close over the years.

Luton didn't have any enemies in Iowa—they said. But how could a man serve as town marshal in one place, even a quiet town like Riddle, for fifteen years—no, twenty-three years now—and not make an enemy? It didn't make sense to Colfax. But if they were right, if Luton had no enemies as town marshal of Riddle, then it had to be someone from Texas—from eight years ago. That meant only Bradley and Simpson. Colfax couldn't come up with any other possibilities.

Milam had said that they could be found up in the Choctaw Nation. *The Choctaw Nation,* he thought. *Damn me. I wonder if that young punk whose gang we wiped out up there is still in jail. What was his name? Collins. That's it. Collins. Brad. Yeah. Brad Collins. That's it. If he's out, there's another possibility. Me and old Sarge really gave them what-for. Bradley, Simpson, Collins.* All trails led to the Choctaw Nation.

He decided to ride on into Henrietta and get a room in a hotel for the night. He'd have a good meal, get a bath and good night's sleep. In the morning he'd head north. *Bradley, Simpson, Collins.*

Simpson and Bradley sat in a small café in Perryville in the Choctaw Nation. They were slurping coffee and smoking. Neither had much to say to the other. They were between jobs. Not broke, but they were running uncomfortably low on cash. Simpson's back was to the door, so it was Bradley who saw the man come in and walk straight toward their table. Simpson could see Bradley stiffen slightly, see the hand slide under the table, ready to go for the gun. Simpson's body underwent a sympathetic stiffening, but he kept himself from turning around to see who was coming. He looked Bradley in the eyes instead, watching for any reaction there. Then, with his peripheral vision, he saw the man walk up beside him and stop beside the table. Then he looked up at him. He didn't appear to have any immediate devilry in mind. Bradley relaxed a bit. Then so did Simpson.

"You two Bradley and Simpson?" said the newcomer.

"Who'd be wanting to know?" said Bradley.

Simpson's eyes narrowed, and he looked sideways at the stranger, who just smiled and continued to talk easy.

"My name's Brad Collins," he said. "Can I sit down?"

"Sit," said Bradley. "I'm Jordan Bradley, and this here is Simpson."

"Yeah," said Collins.

"What're you looking us up for?" said Simpson, his eyes still narrow.

Collins slid down in his chair until he rested on his spine.

"Someone told me who you was," he said. "Said you might be interested in making some easy money. Fast. Said you was game, too."

"That all depends," said Bradley. "What's the deal?"

"Three-way split," said Collins. "That's generous, 'cause I'm the one who knows what the job is. Got it all figured out. But I need some help, so I have to be generous. My old gang got wiped out here about eight years ago. I just got out of the jail house myself. I'm dead broke, and I'm raring to go. What do you say?"

"You never said what the job was," said Simpson.

"Oh, yeah."

Collins leaned in close and lowered his voice.

"The Choctaws is getting a big claim settlement from the government. One hundred and ten thousand dollars. In silver."

Simpson whistled through his teeth.

"When?" said Bradley.

"Day after tomorrow."

"How's it coming?"

"By choo-choo train. Well?"

Bradley smiled, and Simpson, picking up the cue, grinned.

"I'd drink to that," said Bradley, "if I knew where to get a drink in this godforsaken Indian Territory."

"You got the money, I know the place," said Collins.

54

"Let's go."

George Fisher opened the front door of the Cross Timbers Hotel and stepped inside. Ryan came in just behind him, staying two paces to Fisher's rear and one to his left. Emily looked up from behind the counter.

"George," she said, "how dare you come back here after what you did to my father? Get out and take your pet dog with you."

Ryan's face colored, but he kept quiet. Fisher moved toward the counter.

"I just came to take you home, honey," he said. "It's been a long time, and I've come a long ways for you and young Matt."

"Stay where you are," said Emily.

Fisher took another step toward the counter.

"Let's just forget all about the past," he said. "We're a family. You're my wife."

"I'm your ex-wife, and that's the way it's going to stay."

"Well, Matt's my son."

"But I have court-awarded custody. Now get out."

Fisher moved toward the counter again.

"What God hath joined together," he said, "let no man put asunder."

"George," said Emily, raising her voice, "you leave me alone. You hear? Leave me alone. Get out of here."

"I'll never leave you alone, Mrs. Fisher. Never. You're going back to Boston with me on the next train out of here. You and Matt."

Fisher was within two strides of the counter when Matt stepped out on the top landing of the stairs and, taking in the situation quickly, shouted back over his shoulder.

"Grandpa!"

Fisher stopped and looked up at Matt, who was running down the stairs. Matt hurried over to his mother's side and put an arm around her, staring defiantly at the man he knew was his father.

"You get out of here and leave my mother alone," he said.

Fisher smiled.

"That makes a nice picture," he said. "Mother and son. The only thing is, Father should be in that picture, too. Come on. Let's go."

The smile was gone from Fisher's face, and Emily knew that he was through talking. He was about to do something. She clutched Matt to her with all her strength.

"We're not going anywhere with you," she said.

"You touch my mother and I'll kill you," said Matt.

Fisher paused.

"I see that I'm going to have to teach both of you some manners," he said.

Then he nodded over his shoulder toward Ryan.

"Bring them along."

Ryan reached inside his coat and pulled out a Smith and Wesson Pocket .38, but just as he started to move toward the counter, Hal Decker appeared on the top landing, a Remington 10-gauge shotgun with 28-inch barrels clutched in his hands and pointed at Ryan. Both hammers were already pulled back.

"Get the goddamed hell out of my hotel, you sonofabitches," he shouted.

Ryan hesitated an instant, then swung the .38 toward Decker. Decker aimed the shotgun at the floor between the two men and pulled one trigger. The major impact of the blast hit the floor harmlessly, but both Ryan and Fisher were stung by a number of peripheral and ricocheting pellets. Ryan screamed, dropped his .38, and clutched at a particularly bad bite in his left arm. Blood ran between his fingers and down his sleeve. Fisher hollered and made a dive for the door. When Ryan discovered that his boss had abandoned him to the second vicious barrel, he, too, bolted for the door. Decker quickly replaced the spent shell, then made his way down the stairs to join his daughter and grandson behind the counter.

"Dad," said Emily.

"Hush. Both of you get down behind the counter. They'll be back."

"But, Grandpa," said Matt, "Ryan dropped his gun."

"Yeah?"

"Yeah," said Matt, running to retrieve the .38 from the floor. "Here it is." He ran back around the counter to stand beside Decker, and he placed the .38 on the countertop.

"Well," said Decker, "you hang on to it."

"Dad—"said Emily.

"He's old enough. Besides, this is an emergency. Well, at least they won't be back until they can find themselves another weapon."

Across the street from the Cross Timbers, Red Squiers, sheriff of Henrietta, was walking down the sidewalk when he heard the shotgun blast. He turned toward the noise in time to see a stranger dive through the front door of the hotel and go rolling in the street. A few seconds later another man, this one clutching a bloody arm, ran out into the street and tripped over the first one. Squiers jerked out his Colt Sheriff's Model Peacemaker .45 and ran toward the ruckus.

Fisher kicked at Ryan angrily and clambered to his feet. Ryan raised himself painfully to his knees, still holding his bleeding arm.

"Mr. Fisher," he said, "I've been shot."

Before Fisher had time to respond, Red Squiers was standing in front of the two men, gun in hand.

"All right," he said, "what's going on here?"

Fisher saw the star on the man's chest, and he thought fast.

"That crazy old fool in there just took a shot at us," he said. "He wounded Mr. Ryan, here."

"Mr. Ryan, eh?" said Squiers. "And who might you be?"

"Why, I'm George Fisher of Fisher Limited in Boston."

Fisher reached into an inside coat pocket and produced a card, which he presented to the sheriff. Squiers took it, squinted at it, and poked it into a vest pocket.

"Boston, is it?" he said. "Well, you two just stay right here while I have a little chat with Hal Decker."

Squiers started toward the door, but just then Decker stepped into the doorway. He still held the long-barreled Remington.

"Hello, Hal," said Squiers.

"Howdy, Red."

"What happened here?"

"Those two tried to kidnap my daughter and my grandson. They're the same two that beat me up. I stopped them this time. That's all."

Squiers turned back toward Ryan and Fisher.

"What do you two have to say about that?"

"He shot at us," said Fisher. "We're not even armed."

Matt squeezed between the doorjamb and his grandfather to stand on the sidewalk.

"They're not now," he said, "because Ryan dropped this when Grandpa shot him."

He held out the .38 for the sheriff to see.

"That's right," said Decker. "That's his gun."

"Well, that's my wife in there," said Decker. Pointing at Matt, he added, "And that's my son. I'm just trying to take them home."

"That's a half-truth, Red," said Decker, stepping out onto the sidewalk to stand beside Matt. "My daughter divorced that man over eight years ago because he was a wife beater. The court gave her custody of the boy. He's got no claim on either one of them."

Squiers pointed his Peacemaker at Fisher's chest.

"Mr. Boston," he said, "I don't like men that beats women. I want you out of town on the next train."

"I've already got the tickets," said Fisher.

"And between now and then, if I hear you've even come close to the Cross Timbers Hotel, or Mr. Decker here, or Miss Emily or young Matthew, I'll throw your Yankee ass in jail. You got that?"

"I understand you clearly, Sheriff," said Fisher, dusting off his trousers.

"Then get going. Both of you."

Fisher started down the street, followed by Ryan. Squiers and

Decker watched them for a while, then Squiers dropped the Peacemaker back into its holster.

"Thanks, Red," said Decker.

"You said eight years, Hal?" said Squiers, scratching his head.

"That's right."

"What would make a man come after an ex-wife and a kid after eight years?" Emily stepped into the doorway from inside the hotel.

"I think I can answer that, Mr. Squiers," she said. "He must have read *The Police Gazette.*"

"Huh?"

"Eight years ago a man named Bluff Luton promised me that George would never bother me again. He didn't until now. Mr. Luton was recently killed in Iowa, and the story was reported in the *Gazette*. George must have read it. I don't know what Mr. Luton did or said to keep George away from me, but it doesn't matter anymore, does it? He's gone now."

Squiers shook his head.

"Well," he said, "if he gives you any more trouble, you just let me know." Squiers turned to walk toward his office, and Decker turned to usher Emily through the door before him. As Matt turned to follow, he noticed a man sitting on a horse at the hitch rail just down from the hotel. The man was watching them. Something about him was vaguely familiar to Matt. Then his eyes found the big Colt strapped high on his waist and slightly to the front. He turned and ran into the hotel behind his grandfather, then rushed over to his mother.

"Mom," he said. "Mom. There's a man out there in the street. Come over here. Can you see him?"

Emily followed Matt to the window and tried to look out without being observed from outside.

"Yes," she said, "I think so. Just down at the rail?"

"Yeah. Mom? Is that Mr. Colfax?"

The sight of the man brought a flood of memories to Emily's mind. This was the man who had dogged Luton's trail for so long, the man Luton had gotten sick of seeing, the man who had vowed that he would kill Luton. It was also the man who had in spite of himself grown to like Luton, and the man of whom Luton had written, ". . . somehow I can't stop myself from liking the man."

She stepped away from the window with the uneasy feeling that, her precautions notwithstanding, Colfax had known she was watching him.

"Why, I believe it is," she said, finally answering her son's question. "I wonder how long he's been sitting there."

Chapter Nine

Colfax climbed down off his mount and stretched. He gave the animal's reins a couple of turns around the hitch rail, glanced up at the sign that read CROSS TIMBERS HOTEL, and stepped up onto the sidewalk. He had remembered from eight years past that the young woman on the train, the divorced woman with the small son whom Luton had been protecting, had come here, and he had casually wondered if she would still be around. Likely, he had thought, she would have moved on by now. She was a good-looking woman. Some man probably had happened along and latched on to her right away. Even with the kid. He had been surprised eight years ago when Luton had ridden off and left her. He had felt sure that Luton had fallen for the woman. *Hell,* he thought, *now I recall, I even accused him to his face of falling in love. Well, if she had married Bluff Luton, she'd be a widow woman today.*

So he had come to the Cross Timbers on the off chance that he might see her—one more person from Luton's past.

Then when he had ridden up to the rail just down from the front door of the hotel, he had witnessed a minor confrontation. A shotgun blast had driven two man—Easterners from their looks—out of the hotel. The sheriff had come running from across the street, and the man with the shotgun had come out the front door of the hotel. He had been followed by a strapping young boy and then by the woman. She was the one. He'd have recognized her anywhere. Then he decided that the young man must be the kid grown-up—or almost grown. He hadn't realized until then just how long eight years was. He looked again at the eastern dudes, and then he recognized the one Luton had pitched off the train back then, and suddenly he realized that he had a new suspect. This thing was becoming complicated. Luton had been killed in Iowa, probably by someone from his past in Texas. Up until this moment Colfax had believed that the only two real possibilities were the leftover "range detectives," Bradley and Simpson, or the Indian Territory ruffian, Brad Collins. He had forgotten this Easterner, this dude Luton had thrown headlong from a moving train to protect a lady. Now there were three trails.

He pushed open the front door of the Cross Timbers and stepped inside. He saw the old man, still cautious, behind the counter holding that long-barreled shotgun. The woman (he couldn't remember her name) stood at the end of the counter near the bottom of the stairway, her son close by her side. Colfax looked back at the old man and held his hands out to his sides, palms up.

"I'm just looking for a room for the night," he said.

The old man put the shotgun down behind the counter and spun his hotel register around.

"Sign here," he said. "Sorry about the gun. We just had a little trouble here."

Colfax stepped over to the counter to sign the book.

"I saw some of it," he said.

The hotel man spun the book back around and read the newly inscribed name.

He looked his latest customer in the eyes.

"Oliver Colfax," he said. "Welcome to the Cross Timbers

Hotel, Mr. Colfax. I'm Hal Decker. This is my daughter, Emily, and her son, Matt."

"I knew it was Mr. Colfax," said Matt.

"Hello," said Emily. "We've met before."

"Yes," said Colfax, "a few years ago. This young man was much smaller then."

Matt ducked his head as Emily put an arm around his shoulders.

"He has grown up," she said, "hasn't he?"

Colfax took off his hat and dropped it on the counter. The rattlesnake tail on his hatband jiggled, and Matt stared at it. Colfax, too, stared at the hat for a few seconds before glancing back up toward Emily.

"It seems to me that I recognized one of those two men out there in the street," he said.

"That was Ryan," said Matt.

"You saw him on the train, Mr. Colfax," said Emily, "before Mr. Luton threw him off."

"I thought so. Who was the other one?"

"That was George Fisher. My ex-husband."

"My father," said Matt with obvious disgust in his voice.

"Has he been bothering you all these years?"

"We ain't seen or heard nothing of him for eight years," said Hal Decker. "Not until now."

The information Colfax was getting piecemeal was thus far what he had expected to hear, but he needed to know more. He wasn't at all sure what Emily Fisher and her son thought of him. The last they had known, he was planning to kill Bluff Luton himself, but he had to have information, so he had to keep trying.

"Well," he said, "why do you figure he left you alone all this time and just now decided to come after you?"

Emily felt her face flush just a bit, but she took a deep breath, straightened herself, and stepped toward Colfax.

"Mr. Colfax," she said, "Mr. Luton appointed himself my protector—mine and Matt's—while we were on the train."

"I noticed that," said Colfax.

"He promised me before he left here that George would never bother us again, and everything was all right until—until Mr. Luton was murdered."

"So you heard about that, too?" said Colfax.

"Yes."

Colfax looked around the hotel lobby and saw some lounge furniture in one corner of the room.

"I hope you don't think I'm asking too many questions about things that are none of my business," he said. "I do have an interest in all this. Could we sit down over here and talk?"

"Certainly," said Emily.

"Oh, excuse me. I should find a place to get my horse boarded."

"I'll take him for you," said Matt.

"Thank you."

Hal Decker squinted at Colfax as Matt ran for the front door to get the horse and take it to the stable.

"Emily," he asked, "is this the man Luton mentioned in his letter?"

"Yes, Dad," she said. "Let's sit down."

They moved over to the lounge area of the lobby, where Decker and Emily sat down at opposite ends of the same couch. Colfax took an easy chair that faced them.

"Have you had a letter from Bluff Luton?" he asked.

"You said you have an interest, Mr. Colfax," said Emily. "Suppose you explain that to us before we answer any more of your questions. I don't mean to be rude."

Colfax smiled. He knew that to anyone who had known him eight years ago, the role he was now playing would seem an unlikely one. Yet how could he explain it to anyone? How could he tell anyone that he, once a notorious professional killer, had changed so much because he had known Bluff Luton? Could he tell them that he had been able to follow his callous chosen profession because of a philosophy, supported by his reading of Shakespeare, that told him mankind was intrinsically evil and therefore deserving of untimely death? And that Luton had forced him to re-examine that philosophy? Could he say that Bluff Luton was the first good man he had known? And if he could say all this, would anyone believe him? He looked straight at Emily.

"I took a liking to Sarge," he said, "and when I heard that he'd been killed, I vowed to find the man that did it—and kill him."

Emily studied Colfax for a moment. He was calm and still.

"I believe you," she said. "He was—a very likable man."

Colfax thought that he could see Emily's eyes develop a sudden dampness, but she held back the tears, if tears they were, and continued.

"What questions do you have?"

"Could Fisher have killed Sarge—or had him killed?"

Emily seemed startled by the question. She thought for a moment before answering.

"I hadn't even considered that possibility, Mr. Colfax," she said. "I don't know. I didn't think that George even knew who Mr. Luton was. Of course, Ryan saw him on the train, but Ryan never heard his name that I recall. I just assumed that Ryan saw the article and recognized the portrait in *The Police Gazette* and told George about it. But Mr. Luton had to have done something to make George leave me alone. He might have identified himself to George. I don't know."

"Then it is a possibility," said Colfax.

"I suppose so."

"What about the letter?" said Colfax.

"What?"

"You got a letter from Bluff."

"Oh, yes," said Emily.

"He asked her to marry him," said Decker, pleased to find a place where he could jump into the conversation. "After eight years of not even writing, he popped the question. Surprised the hell out of us. And she said yes. Then he got himself killed."

Colfax put a hand to his brow.

"I'm sorry," he said. "I had no idea. Eight years ago I thought

65

that he might ask you, but after all this time—I had no idea. This must all be very difficult for you. I'm sorry."

"It's all right, Mr. Colfax. I'm glad you're here, and I'm glad to know what it is you're up to. I hope you succeed. It may be wrong of me, but whoever murdered Mr. Luton took something away from me that I wanted very badly. I hope you find him."

"I intend to," said Colfax. "I, uh, I went out and visited his grave earlier today."

"What?"

"I just said that I went out to Will Milam's ranch to visit the grave. It just seemed like the thing to do, I guess."

"They sent the body down here?" said Decker.

"Why, yes. Didn't you know?"

Matt Fisher knew little about Oliver Colfax. He remembered the look of the man. He remembered particularly the rattles on the hatband and the big Colt worn high on the waist and around toward the front. He knew that Luton had written to his mother that he liked the mysterious man, and he associated Colfax closely in his mind with Luton. Therefore he was excited to have Colfax in town and at his grandfather's hotel, and he was pleased and proud to have taken Colfax's horse to the stable for him. He shoved his hands in his pockets, held his head high, and strutted as he walked back toward the Cross Timbers.

He rounded the corner just down from the stable and stepped off the sidewalk before he saw that he had come to its end. He stumbled slightly, regained his composure, and started to strut again. The sun had just gone down, and the alley he was about to cross was dark. He felt a big hand clap itself over his mouth and nose and pull him backward against a body. He flailed his arms and kicked behind him with his feet. Then he felt a sharp, metallic point against his throat, and he ceased his kicking and flailing. He felt hot breath against the side of his face, and he smelled a strange man smell, close and overpowering. A raspy voice sounded in his ear, and he recognized it as belonging to Ryan.

"Keep still or I'll cut your throat. Now walk."

Ryan forced Matt through the dark alley and into a back door of Hal Decker's nearest competitor. They stumbled awkwardly up the stairs, Ryan still clutching Matt tightly against his own body. Matt could smell the man's breath, and he thought that he was going to be sick. They reached a door on the second floor, and Ryan inserted a skeleton key in the lock. He opened the door and gave Matt a shove.

"Inside," he said. "Mr. Fisher, look what I brought you."

George Fisher, stretched out on the bed, raised his head up from the pillow.

When he saw Matt, he quickly sat up on the edge of the bed and smiled.

"Hello, son," he said.

Chapter Ten

The place was only a couple of miles outside of Perryville. It was a small frame house in the woods, set back a ways from the road, a private residence, the home of a white man. He might have been a Choctaw mixed-blood citizen, a white man married to an Indian woman, a renter or a squatter. No one seemed to know, but Brad Collins knew all he wanted to know about the man. From him one could purchase homemade whiskey or Choctaw beer in any quantity at any time, and it was to this place that Collins had led Jordan Bradley and Simpson in order to drink and to plan. They bought a jug of whiskey from the man and found a big pecan tree nearby under which to sit. Bradley, who had paid for the jug, took the first sip and passed it to Simpson.

"Goddamn," he said. "Nobody would ever call that shit smooth."

Simpson took a great gulp, smacked his lips, and passed the jug to Brad Collins.

"That's some better," said Simpson.

Collins took his turn, then set the jug down in the dirt where any one of the three who wanted it could reach it.

"It ain't the best stuff available around here," he said, "but it's the clostest."

"That's all right with me," said Simpson, reaching for the jug.

"How's this job going to work?" said Bradley.

Collins sat up straight, crossing his legs in front of himself. He pushed his hat back on his head and leaned confidentially toward Bradley and Simpson. Although there was no one else near, he spoke in a low voice.

"Well," he said, "I'll tell you. The train will come through Perryville tomorrow at noon. Just south of town there's a steep grade that will slow it down. We'll be there."

He pointed at Simpson.

"You'll be at the top of that hill. Bradley, you'll be down at the bottom of the grade. I'll be halfway up—in between the two of you. When the train gets to chugging up that grade, it'll slow it down considerable. I'll hop on. The silver's going to be on the last car. Nothing behind it but just the caboose. I'll unhook them two cars. The train will keep going—I think. I don't think they'll even notice, but just in case they do, that's what you're up there on top of the hill for. If they don't just keep going, you fire a shot to warn us."

He reached down for the jug and tipped it up to his lips.

"What about me?" said Bradley.

"The two cars I cut loose will just roll back down, and you'll be there waiting for them. Simpson will have his horse with him up on top. Soon as he's sure the train's gone on its way, he'll ride on down to join us. Our horses'll be down there with you. I'll ride the cars down."

Simpson gave Bradley a questioning look and waited. Bradley picked up a twig from the ground, bit the end off it, and spat it out.

"What do we do if you're wrong?" he said. "What do we do if we hear Simpson's warning shot and that train's coming back?"

Collins looked at Simpson.

"You have to fire that warning shot, you get right on back down to the bottom of the hill. I'll get my ass down there, too, and we'll scoot. That's all. We won't be no broker than we are now."

Bradley ran his tongue between his upper lip and his teeth. He stared at the jug on the ground for a moment before he spoke again.

"Sounds all right so far," he said.

"So far," echoed Simpson.

"We get the silver," said Bradley, "where do we go?"

"We follow the tracks north across the border into the Creek Nation and on to Eufala. I've got a friend there we can stay with. Then we figure it from there."

"Three-way split?" said Bradley.

"Three-way."

"We'll do it."

Emily shot her father an inquisitive look. The only response she got from him was a shrug of the shoulders. She took a deep breath and looked back at Colfax.

"Mr. Colfax," she said, "did I understand you right? Did you just say that you visited Mr. Luton's grave out at Will Milam's ranch?"

"Why, yes," said Colfax. He was puzzled at her reaction. It was almost as if he had done something wrong. "Surely you've been out to see it yourself."

"No, I have not," said Emily. "As far as I knew, Mr. Luton was buried up in Iowa. I've not had any word from anyone since I last wrote him. I read about his death, as you did, in *The Police Gazette*. I suppose I really shouldn't blame Mr. Milam. He had no idea of our plans. I haven't seen him since my brief correspondence with Mr. Luton."

Colfax felt uneasy. This was to him a totally new way of dealing with death—a thing he had dealt with in other ways many times over. He caught himself fidgeting with his hat brim. He dropped the hat to the floor beside his chair.

"Miz, uh, Fisher," he said.

"Please call me Emily."

"Emily, would you like to ride out there in the morning? I'd be happy to accompany you."

"Thank you, Mr. Colfax," she said. "I would like that."

Just then the door was thrown open from the outside, and a scrawny, towheaded lad came bursting into the room. He was clutching a piece of ｊpaper in his right hand.

"Miz Fisher?" he said.

Emily stood up and walked toward the boy.

"I'm Mrs. Fisher," she said. "What can I do for you?"

"A man told me to give you this."

He held the paper out toward Emily.

"He gave me a quarter," he said.

Emily took the paper out of the grubby little hand and tried to smooth its wrinkles.

"Thank you," she said, and the boy turned and ran out the door, not thinking to close it behind himself. Emily, reading the paper, followed in the boy's tracks and closed the door. Then, having finished reading what was written on the piece of paper in her hand, she turned and leaned heavily against the big door.

"My God," she said.

"What is it?" said Hal Decker. "Who's it from?"

"It's from George," said Emily. "He's got Matt."

Hal Decker sprang from his seat and ran over to his daughter. He tore the note from her hand. Colfax stood up but remained by the chair in which he had been sitting. Decker read through the note.

"That no-good bastard," he said.

"What does it say?" asked Colfax.

Decker held the note up in front of his face to read it once more.

"Says, 'My dear Emily, don't go for the sheriff. Ryan and I have already left the hotel. We have Matt with us. If you ever hope to see him again, you will do exactly as I say. I know you can drive a buggy. Get one and follow the map on this paper to the shack. Come alone. We can see from this place for a long distance, so I'll know if anyone is with you. Be there by noon tomorrow, or else. George.'"

Colfax walked over to the old man and held out his hand.

"May I?" he said.

Decker handed the note to Colfax, who studied the crudely drawn map at the bottom of the page.

"I know that place," he said. "I stayed there once myself. It's an abandoned line shack on Will Milam's ranch. Off by itself. He's right. You can see anyone who's coming from there. The land around it's as flat as this floor."

"How the hell did George Fisher ever find a place like that around here?" asked Decker.

"Ryan must have found it for him somehow," said Emily. "He makes Ryan do all his chores for him."

"It doesn't matter how he found the place," said Colfax. "What matters is how we can get to them to get your boy back safely."

"He said I have to come alone."

"I know what the note says, but I just dealt myself in. Trust me. This is my kind of work."

The visit to the grave will have to wait, thought Colfax, *and so will my trip up to the Choctaw Nation.*

"What are you going to do, Colfax?" said Decker.

"I'm going to do what Sarge should have done in the first place. I'm going to kill them both. Where can we rent a buggy in this town?"

"Down to the livery. Where Matt took your horse," said Decker.

"Let's take a walk down there."

"Now?" said Decker.

"Right now."

Chapter Eleven

Blue Steele sat at the table in his kitchen. Breakfast was done and the table had been cleared. His wife, Maribel, was brushing his long, straight hair. Blue's mind was on the murders. Only one of them, that of Fields, was officially his business, but he was convinced that the killings were somehow related. He couldn't come up with any connection between Sergeant Bluff Luton and Lance Fields other than the way in which they had been killed, but that in itself was enough to convince him of a connection. There had been no murders in either town for eight years—since Blue had become town marshal of West Riddle. Suddenly there had been two—one on each side of the river. Both men had been shot in the back, apparently with a rifle of the same caliber. They must be related, he thought.

"Ow."

He felt the brush pull through a stubborn tangle of hair.

"Sorry," said Maribel.

"It's okay."

"I always thought your hair was black."

"It *is* black."

"It's brown. Real dark brown, but it's brown. I can see it in this light."

"It's always been black. I ought to know."

"And," said Maribel, "I'm standing here looking at it. I'm brushing it, and it's brown."

"Dammit," said Blue, shoving his chair suddenly away from the table and standing up. "I know the color of my own damn hair. It's black. It's always been black. Damn."

Blue Steele stalked across the room as Maribel tossed the brush down on the table. She put her hands on her hips and glared at her husband's back. "Well, bite my head off, then," she said.

Blue rubbed his forehead with his left hand and sighed. He felt foolish. "I'm sorry," he said. "I didn't mean to. I'm thinking about those killings, and I'm afraid they've got me stumped. Dammit. I don't like the feeling."

He turned to face Maribel and held out his arms to her. She gave him a suspicious look, hesitated, then walked into his embrace. He held her close for a few seconds, kissed her on the cheek, and then released her.

"I better get going," he said.

As he walked across the room to pick up his hat, he glanced in a mirror hanging on the wall. He slowed down and gave himself a long look. *Damn,* he said to himself, it *is* brown.

Victor Bragg was about to leave for the bank when his wife, Ruth, stopped him and straightened his tie even though it really looked perfectly all right. She had a worried look on her face. The furrowed brows and the tightly drawn lips pained Victor Bragg. He put his hands on her shoulders and kissed her on the forehead.

"Everything will be just fine, Ruth," he said.

"I'm so worried about him, Victor."

"He's safe."

He wished that he could tell her how safe the boy was—how he knew he was safe.

"But he hasn't left the house since—well, since that night."

Bragg paced away from his wife. He shoved his hands into his pockets and pursed his lips.

"I know, Ruthie," he said. "I know. I'll have a talk with him."

"Now?"

He looked at her. He hated to see her so worried. He had always protected her. He could protect her from everything else—everything except the worry she suffered over their son. *Damn him*, thought Bragg. *How did he ever grow up to be so damn useless? What did I do wrong?* He took a deep breath and walked in long strides to the door to Stan's room. With the back of his hand he rapped on the door.

"Stanley?"

Receiving no answer, he opened the door and stepped inside. Stanley Bragg was sitting on the edge of the bed. He had pulled on his trousers but wore no shirt or boots. He hadn't shaved for several days. He didn't look up when his father came into the room. The elder Bragg cleared his throat loudly and self-consciously. Stanley glanced up at him, then away again.

"Stan?"

Stanley stared at the floor.

"Stan, you've got to get out of the house. You can't just keep on sitting in here like this. Your mother's worried about you, son."

"Yeah?" said Stan. "Well, she's got reason. My best friend was shot in the back and killed. I was right beside him. That damn Indian lawman across the river, he said the killer might have shot the wrong man."

"What?"

"What if the bastard was trying to kill me and shot Lance by mistake? Huh? He might try to get me again."

"That's absurd," said Victor Bragg.

"What's so absurd about it?"

"Why," said Victor, "who would want to kill you?"

"I don't know. I don't know, but who would want to kill

Lance? I don't know that, either, but someone did."

"Son, get dressed and come to the bank with me today, will you?"

"No, sir. I ain't budging from this house, and I've got my gun loaded and handy, too."

Bragg wanted to slap his son across the face, but he knew that would do no good.

"You mean to tell me," he said, "that you're staying in this house because you're afraid that some killer might come after you?"

"Yes."

"And you would sit here in this house and endanger your mother?"

"What? What do you mean?"

Bragg had him now. He had to keep jabbing.

"If there is someone after you, which I doubt very much, but if there is and you stay here at home all the time, he'll have to come looking for you here, and then your mother will be in danger, too. Is that what you want? Is that all the bigger a man you are?"

"I—I didn't think of that. Dad, I'm scared. I don't know what to do."

"Get dressed," said Bragg, feeling marvelously triumphant. "I'll wait for you, and we'll ride on into the bank together. You can wear your gun. If it'll make you feel better, I'll even wear one today. All right?"

"All right," said Stan. "All right. I'll be ready in a minute. Wait for me. Okay?"

"All right, son. I'll just be out here with your mother."

Colfax had thought he would be able to curl up on the floor of the buggy Emily would drive out to the line shack, but when he had taken a good look at the buggy, he had concluded that it wasn't going to work. The floor space was too cramped. By the time he got to the shack, he'd have been too stiff to be able to move quickly. Besides that, he wouldn't be as well concealed from view as he had imagined. He hated to give that damned Bostonian any credit, but it did seem as if his insistence that Emily drive a buggy had been a reasonably smart move. He'd had to come up with a new plan, and he had decided that as flat as the damned North Texas plain was, a man could sneak still up on that shack in the dark.

He had arranged for the buggy to be delivered to the Cross Timbers first thing in the morning for Emily. She was to follow the directions given on the note to the line shack, just as she had been instructed. He had told Decker to give Emily an hour's start, then to go to the sheriff and tell him the whole story. Then he had sent them to bed, and he had gone back to the stable for his horse. So much for the night's rest in a hotel bed he had planned on before his trip to the Choctaw Nation. He had ridden as close to the shack as he dared, then dismounted and continued on foot. When he had gotten close enough to the shack to see the light coming from inside, he'd dropped down on his belly and crawled. The worst of it was when he found himself in the middle of patches of sticker burrs and goatheads. The damned things stabbed deep, and they hurt. He stopped crawling now and then, to pull the vicious little devils out of his flesh. He had made it to the shack without being seen and had crawled on to the outhouse that stood behind it. Behind the outhouse, he settled down to wait.

Deputy United States Marshal Oren Reid sat impatiently sipping coffee in the Perryville hash house. He pulled the watch from his vest pocket and, checking the time, realized that he was early. That realization irritated Reid. He had preferred the feeling that he was being made to wait for an Indian who was late. He had it firmly in his mind that an Indian would always be late, and he liked having his preconceptions confirmed. He shoved the watch back into his pocket as the front door opened, and a dark-skinned man in a blue uniform walked in. Reid tried to act as if he hadn't noticed as the Indian walked over to his table.

"Deputy Marshal Reid?" said the Indian.

"I'm Reid."

The Indian held out a dark hand, which Reid reluctantly and briefly gripped. He was disgusted by the Indian's limp handshake.

"I'm Captain Billie of the Choctaw Lighthorse."

"I figured," said Reid.

Captain Billie sat down opposite Reid and took off his cap.

"Deputy Reid," he said, "I asked for help from the federal government because I have reason to believe that a crime is about to be committed that will fall at least partially under your jurisdiction. We have a large payment of silver coming in on the train that will be through here tomorrow at noon."

"One hundred and ten thousand dollars," said Reid. "I know all about that." Reid thought that it was a waste of good money to give it away to Indians. He resented having been sent on this assignment to guard "Indian money" and to work with Indian police, but he would do it. He always did his duty, however unpleasant. There was talk of doing away with these Indian governments and creating a new state out of Indian Territory and Oklahoma Territory, and as far as Reid was concerned, it couldn't happen too soon. Captain Billie continued.

"I believe that the train will be held up just south of here by three men—two white men and one Cherokee citizen. I can arrest the Cherokee, but I can't arrest the white men. That's why I asked for your help."

"What's your source of information?" said Reid.

"It's reliable."

Goddamned secretive Indians, thought Reid. *I'll bet it's reliable.* He knew, though, that he'd have to go along with the Choctaw. He had his orders. Besides, Billie just might be right, and if Reid refused to cooperate, since Billie had made an official request, he would be seen as negligent. Son of a bitch.

"The train will stop briefly in Perryville," said Captain Billie. "I suggest that we get inside the car that carries the money. I have six men. Seven of us and you. We wait for them to strike. I think they'll make this move just south of town on a steep grade where the train will be slowed down. Everything will go their way until they open the door and find us."

"All right," said Reid. "I'll meet you here tomorrow at noon."

"Make it eleven-thirty," said Captain Billie.

Reid let out an exasperated sigh.

"Eleven-thirty," he said.

Coleman J. Miller had just a few minutes earlier opened his store when he heard the tinkle of the bell over his front door. He seldom had customers so early, so he turned toward the noise with some curiosity, only to see the doctor and the undertaker hurrying in together.

"Clarence," he said. "Rudy. What's up?"

"C. J.," said Doc Gallager, "we've got to talk."

"Why, Rudy? Has there been any change?"

Miller moved anxiously toward his visitors, and he thought that he could read anxiety on their faces also.

"Nothing's changed," said Gallager, "but we can't keep this up indefinitely."

"It's making a nervous wreck out of me," said Clarence Dry. "We've got to let it out."

"We can't," said Miller. "Dammit, we've been all over this before. We agreed. Remember? There's good reason."

"We didn't know it would drag on so long," said the doctor. "I couldn't tell. I thought we'd know something one way or the other by now—but there's no change."

"Yes. You said that."

"C. J., listen to me," said Dry, but Miller hushed him with an impatient gesture and a hard glance.

"Just—just be quiet for a minute," he said. "Both of you. Look here. You said it yourselves. Nothing has changed. And that's my answer. Nothing has changed. You understand me? Do we understand one another? All right?"

Dry and Gallager looked at each other, then, almost in unison, at the floor. When the front doorbell sounded again, Miller wasn't surprised. He was facing the door and saw the man coming in, but the other two were startled by the sound. They looked around to see Blue Steele coming into the store. Miller shot a quick look at his companions, which told them to keep their opinions to themselves. Then he smiled.

"Hello, Blue," he said. "What brings you across the river so early this morning?"

"Morning, Mr. Miller," said Steele. "Mr. Dry. Doc Gallager. Ah, I, uh, it's those killings, Mr. Miller. They keep nagging at me. I thought I'd come on back over here and poke around some more."

Something's not quite right here, Steele told himself. The last time he had come to see Miller, these same two had been with him. They seemed nervous, secretive somehow. Then and now. And he thought that he had seen a quick warning look flash from Miller to the others just as he had walked through the door. He moved on through the store to the counter in back, where the three were huddled.

"What more do you think that you can find out here?" asked Miller. "We've told you all we can about the Luton . . . shooting. And you've talked to young Bragg. You think he didn't tell you everything he knows?"

Steele took off his hat and scratched his head.

"I don't think anything about anyone, Mr. Miller," he said, "but everything seems to point me in this direction. Sarge and Fields were shot by the same rifle."

"We don't really know that, do we?"

"No, but it sure seems like a reasonable thing to believe. Same kind of wound, Doc says. Right, Doc?"

"Very similar, yes," said Gallager.

"Both shot in the back and right close together in time. That after eight years of no killings in either town. I'd say the same killer did both jobs."

"All right," said Miller, "but one was shot on your side of the river, the other on ours. What makes you say everything points you over here?"

"Well, sir, it seems to me that there's got to be some link somewhere. Fields lived in Nebraska and got himself shot over there. Sarge lived here, and here's where he was shot. But Fields was with Stanley Bragg, and Stanley lives here."

"Well," said Miller, "that's not much to go on, Blue."

"No, sir, but it's all I've got. Is there anything any one of you gentlemen can think of that you didn't tell me before?"

"Sorry, Blue," said Miller. "Not a thing. We were just talking about that ourselves, just before you came in. We couldn't come up with anything."

Steele thought that Miller's answer had come out much too quickly, but he decided not to challenge the man—not just yet. This was awkward. Steele owed a lot to Miller from eight years back, and Miller was probably the single most highly respected citizen of Riddle, Iowa. But Blue Steele had an uncomfortable feeling. *The son of a bitch is lying to me,* he thought, *or at least he's not telling me everything he knows.* He slapped his hat back on his head.

"Well," he said, "I'm going to take a run on over to the bank, and maybe out to the Bragg house. I'd like to talk to both Braggs again—if that's all right with you."

"Sure," said Miller. "Go right ahead. And good luck."

"Yeah. See you."

Steele left the store. As the door closed behind him, Doc Gallager gave Miller a hard look.

"C. J.," he said, "I just don't feel right lying to that boy."

Chapter Twelve

Colfax waited behind the outhouse. As the sun rose higher in the Texas sky, he was glad that the line shack selected by Ryan and Fisher for this rendezvous had been an abandoned one. He wasn't yet quite sure what he was going to do. If he tried to move in on the shack, he might be seen. One of the two men could easily be watching out a window, and even if he managed to duck a shot fired from inside the shack, the boy would be placed in danger. He hadn't even dared to poke his head around for a look at the shack, for fear of being seen. He had formulated a plan only thus far—to get him in his position behind the outhouse, near the shack, near the boy and his kidnappers. And he sat there waiting and wondering. If nothing else, he told himself, when Emily came driving up in the buggy, all attention would be on her and the road behind her. Then he could step out from behind his humble blind and kill them. In the meantime he would wait.

Emily Fisher sat straight in the buggy and drove with skill and determination. The determination was that of a mother intent on protecting her young. She didn't know what Colfax was planning, where he had gone, but she couldn't worry about that. She could hope that he would be there, hope that he'd save her and her son from Fisher and Ryan, but she had to be prepared for the worst. If she had to, to protect Matt, she would go with George. She knew that George would hurt her if he got her under his control again. She knew his depraved mind and his perverted impulses, but she had to protect her son. Matt, she thought, Matt. Oh, God, protect him. Keep him safe. He's got to be safe. Yes, she knew that to keep Matt safe from harm she would go with George again. But only as a last resort; she had another alternative to try first. With her right hand she felt under the folds of her skirt for the Smith and Wesson pocket .38 that lay beside her on the buggy seat, the one that Ryan had dropped on the floor of the Cross Timbers and that her father had said Matt could keep. The boy had left it on the counter when he had gone out to take care of Colfax's horse. Reassured somewhat by the feel of the hard steel there by her side, she snapped the buggy whip over the prancing black gelding to hurry it along its way.

"Come on," she said. "Get along."

Hal Decker stepped into the sheriff's office in Henrietta and found Red Squiers sitting at his desk sipping his morning coffee. The sheriff looked up, surprised at the intrusion.

"Morning, Hal," he said. "What's up? You ain't had no more trouble with them two Bostonians, have you?"

Decker stepped across the room and placed the note from Fisher there on the desk before Squiers's eyes.

"Last night," he said, "Matt went out to the stable. He didn't come back. Pretty soon a snot-nosed kid come in and give this to Emily."

Red Squiers read the note.

"Why the hell didn't you tell me about this last night?"

"Well, read what the goddamn note says, Red. It says, 'Don't get the sheriff.' If those bastards was to see you coming, they'd kill Matt. They would. You don't know George Fisher."

"He's the kid's father, ain't he?"

"He's a crazy, sadistic son of a bitch."

"All right, Hal. All right. So now you're here. Why?"

"Emily's on her way out there right now."

"By herself?"

"That's what the note says, don't it? But listen. Colfax went out there last night. Sneaked out in the dark."

"Hold on," said Red Squiers. "Who the hell is Colfax?"

"Oh, dammit, Red," said Decker, "we ain't got time for all this. We got to follow Emily. She's about halfway out there by now. That's when Colfax said we should follow."

Squiers stood up and banged his fist down on the desk. His coffee cup hopped from the impact.

"Who's Colfax?" he shouted.

"I'll tell you on the way. Let's go."

Blue Steele stepped inside the Riddle Valley Bank. His intention was to have a talk with Victor Bragg, then go look for Stanley. He was pleased to see that both Braggs were in the bank. The elder Bragg was seated behind his big desk in his office, an open office, marked off by large glass windows that rose from about four feet off the floor and up to the ceiling. Steele headed for him first. Victor Bragg stiffened as he saw the half-breed marshal from across the river approaching.

"Steele," he said, "what are you doing back here?"

"Hello, Mr. Bragg," said Steele, removing his hat. "Do you mind if I sit down here and take a few minutes of your time?"

"Well, I—I suppose not," said Bragg. "I *am* busy."

"Aren't we all."

"What's on your mind, Steele?"

"Mr. Bragg, I'm still puzzling over those two recent killings."

"Well, the first one is outside of your jurisdiction," said Bragg. "You should be concentrating on the one that took place on your side of the river."

"I believe the two incidents are related, Mr. Bragg. I believe the same man is guilty of both crimes. I've talked to Mr. Miller about it, and I have his permission to investigate on this side, as well as on mine."

"I see."

"I don't have any new evidence, and I don't have any new questions to ask you. I'm just kind of following up on our last visit. I want to find out if you or anyone else over here has thought of anything—anything at all—to add to what you told me before."

"No, Steele," said Bragg. "I've nothing to add. I can't help you anymore, I'm afraid. The reason I answer so quickly and definitely is that I've given this entire business a great deal of thought since we last talked, and I haven't been able to come up with anything at all."

"All right," said Steele. "Well, if you should think of anything, let me know, will you?"

"Sure."

Steele gestured toward Stanley Bragg, who was working behind a teller's cage. Actually, at the moment he seemed more interested in his father's visitor than in his own work.

"Mind if I talk to Stan for a few minutes?" said Steele.

Bragg let out an exasperated sigh.

"I'd rather you didn't," he said. "Stan's not been taking this well. I only this morning got him out of the house. He's busy, and I'd just as soon keep his mind on his work."

"Well, Mr. Bragg, part of the purpose of this investigation is to make sure we keep Stanley safe. I'm not sure that the killer got the right man when he shot Lance Fields."

Bragg stood up behind his desk and glared at Steele.

"That's ridiculous," he said. "I don't want to be bothered by you anymore, and I don't want Stanley bothered."

"Mr. Bragg, I'm sorry you feel that way, but in a criminal investigation you don't have that choice to make."

"You don't have any authority in this state."

"I have your mayor's assurance of cooperation."

"Oh, yeah?" said Bragg, storming out from behind his desk and going to the hat rack to snatch up his hat. "Well, I'll take care of that right now. I'll just have a talk with C. J. Miller. And I want you to be out of my bank when I get back."

"Have a nice day," said Steele.

As Bragg slammed the front door of the bank behind himself, Steele walked over to the teller's cage.

"Hi, Marshal," said Stanley. Steele could tell that the boy was nervous. Of course he had witnessed his father's anger with Steele. Victor Bragg had made no attempt to conceal it.

"How are you doing, Stan?"

"All right, I guess."

"Your dad seems to think that I ought to stay on my own side of the river. He doesn't think there's anything for me to investigate over here—or anyone to protect."

"But Mr. Luton was killed over here," said Stanley.

"Yeah."

"The same guy done both, didn't he? Luton and Lance?"

"I think so."

"Didn't you tell my old man that Lance might've got it by mistake? That the guy might've been after me?"

"Yeah."

"Marshal, I did, too, but he seems to think that's just stupid. He won't face up to it. Marshal, Mr. Steele, I'm scared. I mean, someone might be out to kill me. He's killed two men already, and I don't even know who he is. I don't know who to watch out for. There ain't nobody to stand up to and fight."

Steele reached through the cage and put a hand on Stan's shoulder.

"I know, Stan," he said. "Just try to keep steady. I'm doing all I can to try to figure this thing out, but I need your help. If you think of anything at all, let me know. Any connection between Sarge Luton and Lance, or Sarge and you. Anyone who'd want to kill you or Lance or Sarge. Anything you remember about the night Lance was killed that you haven't told me before. You think of anything, tell me about it."

"I will," said Stanley. "You can count on that."

* * *

As Blue Steele rode back toward Nebraska he catalogued in his mind the puzzles of the case he was working on. There was, of course, the main question—or questions. Who killed Luton? Who killed Fields? Was it, indeed, the same killer? He thought so, but he couldn't be sure. Then there was the question of motive. With the Fields case, Steele thought, there were any number of possibilities. Fields had been a wild young man. In his short lifetime he had undoubtedly angered a good many men. Often he had been drunk and unruly. He had been a habitual cardplayer. Still, the marshal didn't really believe that some local who had been offended by Fields was the killer. The two murders, he thought, had to tie together in some way. But when he tried to come up with possibilities for the Luton case, he found himself even more in the dark. The man just hadn't seemed to have made any enemies in years, and it didn't make sense to Steele to try to reach back into Luton's dim past for the answers. *No,* he thought, *the answer's got to be right here. Somewhere right in front of me.*

Other questions nagged at him. Was it possible that the target on the night Fields had been killed had been young Bragg? The young man was certainly afraid of that possibility. Of course, it had been Steele who had planted that fear in him, but once planted, it had taken root and grown. On the other hand, the kid's old man was trying to get Steele off the case entirely. He didn't seem worried about his son's safety at all. Perhaps the father simply couldn't imagine that his own son had done anything bad enough to make anyone want to kill him. Perhaps. What other explanation could there be? And Steele's old friend, C. J. Miller, was acting strangely. That simply could be a result of the pressure the man was under as acting marshal of a town with a recent murder on its hands.

Then there had been the strange appearance of Oliver Colfax. Miller had said that Colfax was looking for Luton's killer. It didn't make any sense at all to Steele to think of a hired assassin trying to bring to justice the murderer of a town marshal. Steele had heard of Colfax—a cold and efficient killer who didn't work cheap. Where the hell did he fit into this puzzle? Could he be the killer? If so, why show his face and indicate an interest in the murder? Why make himself so conspicuous? Had he not done that, no one would have connected him in any way with any of this. But his appearance on the scene was certainly interesting. The killings did have the look to Steele of professional jobs. None of the possible answers to his many questions satisfied Blue Steele. *Get the right answer to any one question,* he thought, *it will answer all the others. I know it will.* He turned his horse up onto the river bridge and headed back into West Riddle.

Ryan stood just outside the door of the line shack smoking a black cigar. He was staring off into the vast, open space in the direction of Henrietta. The first thing he saw was a puff of dust on the distant horizon. He squinted his eyes into the bright Texas sunlight and watched as the puff drew closer and grew larger until he could make out a horse and buggy. He fidgeted for a moment longer, thought he could discern a female at the reins, tossed away his stogie, then turned his head to talk over his shoulder into the shack.

"Mr. Fisher," he said, "I think she's coming."

Behind the outhouse, Oliver Colfax heard Ryan's announcement. He slowly slipped his Colt out of its holster and eased back the hammer. Moving gently, he eased up to his feet, his back against the rear wall of the small structure. It's just about killing time, he said to himself.

Inside the line shack, George Fisher stood up from the cot on which he had been lying, stepped quickly over to where Matt sat stiffly in a straight chair, and grabbed the boy roughly by his shirt collar.

"Come on," he said. "Your mama's coming to see us."

Fisher shoved Matt ahead of him to the doorway.

"Ryan," he said, "stand here and hold on to this kid."

"Yes, sir."

Ryan took hold of Matt from behind by both arms and held him in front of him. Matt could feel the fingers dig into his flesh. The buggy drew closer.

"What are you going to do?" said Matt.

"Shut up," said Fisher. "Hold him, Ryan."

"I've got him, Mr. Fisher."

Fisher stepped out away from the shack and stood, hands on hips, waiting for the buggy. Oliver Colfax, accurately conjecturing that both men's attention would be drawn to the approaching buggy, eased himself to the edge of his slight concealment and spied around its edge to take in the situation. He raised up the Colt and held it ready beside his head.

Chapter Thirteen

The hill was steep and the ground rocky, but there was plenty of cover on either side of the tracks in the thick, tangled woods. Brad Collins had secreted himself in some tall grass just at the edge of the thicket. He was fairly close to the rails, and he would be able to move quickly and easily once the train had reached the desired position. He had supervised the placement of both Bradley and Simpson, and he felt sure that everything would go smoothly.

Simpson, nervously, sat on horseback at the top of the hill. He had his gun in hand, waiting for the worst. At the bottom of the hill Bradley, also on horseback, waited back in the brush. The train would be along any minute, and all three men waited anxiously, like actors backstage awaiting their cues. Then they heard the whistle, and each of them, independently, out of sight of each other, stiffened. The moment was upon them.

Bradley, at the bottom of the hill, was the first to see the train. It came puffing furiously down the tracks. He couldn't imagine that anything, much less the short hill ahead, would slow it down.

He relaxed, fully believing that the train would race past the three outlaws and go on to wherever it was going absolutely unmolested. His job, he believed, was over before it had begun. Halfway up the grade, Brad Collins waited, poised for action. The train hit the rise and slowed at once. The engine's puffs and chugs came farther apart as it labored to pull the string of cars which together constituted its long tail on up and over the hill. Simpson caught a glimpse of the fireman furiously shoveling coal. The engineer pulled the chain to blow the whistle once more. Down the hill, Collins waited, crouched like a panther. The mighty train crept up the rise like a snail.

Black smoke belched from the smokestack at regular, but slow-paced, intervals. The noise of the engine, of the wheels on the tracks, and of the various couplings clanking against each other was deafening. A gunshot could not have been heard over the roar. Collins wiped the sweat from his palms on his jeans. He waited.

Suddenly the car was upon him. His homework, his intelligence, and all his instincts told him it was the car that carried the silver. He burst from his hiding place and sprang to the tracks. He made a desperate grab for the ladder rungs on the side of the boxcar just ahead of the car carrying the silver, and he clutched them. His perceptions of the speed at which the train was traveling changed dramatically in that instant. What had seemed a snail's pace suddenly became an almost unimaginable race against time. Collins felt himself jerked from his feet and slung through the air. He clutched at the ladder rung desperately—hung on for his very life. A panicked thought told him that even if he managed to cling to the rung and work his way to the coupling to disengage it, even if he succeeded in performing his task, the car he wanted would be over the top of the hill and the plan thwarted. He struggled against his better judgment and pulled himself aboard. Taking an instant to collect his thoughts and gather his courage, he worked himself around to a position between the two cars, and he managed to free the silver car. He watched the box-car ahead of him top the rise and vanish, descending on the other side of the hill, and he grinned and waved at Simpson just as the silver car he was riding slowed, hesitated, and then started rolling backward down the hill.

Bradley saw the car coming his way, and he jerked out his pistol and cocked it. He held the gun out at arm's length and waited, but the car rolled down the hill and passed him by. He caught a glimpse of Collins, looking sheepish and helpless, riding the runaway car as they shot together back toward Perryville.

"Hey," shouted Bradley.

He looked up the hill and saw Simpson riding down toward him at an insane pace for that rocky, downhill stretch.

"Come on," he shouted.

Simpson lashed at his mount, and as he came alongside Bradley, Bradley whipped up his own animal in an attempt to catch up with and ride alongside Simpson. He was unsuccessful. Simpson stayed ahead. The train car carrying Collins, and presumably the silver, rolled casually on ahead of both riders. Collins, hanging on to the end of the car, frantically waved his cohorts on. On down the track toward Perryville was a slight grade, almost imperceptible in comparison to the one the car had just raced down backward, but it was enough to slow the pace of the car once again. Again the car hesitated. Again it reversed its course. Bradley and Simpson rode past it before they realized what had happened. By the time they managed to turn their horses around, the silver car carrying Collins had rocked to a halt. Collins jumped down from his perch, pulled two pistols from his belt, and ran around to face the door on the side of the car.

"Open up," he shouted.

Bradley and Simpson came riding up to halt their mounts, one on each side of Collins. They jerked out their revolvers. Then, with an awful roar that disturbed the sudden though brief silence, the door to the car slid open, and there were seven blue-uniformed Indians and one white man, all with weapons leveled at the outlaws. There was an instant of silence again as the outlaws registered shock and dismay, and hesitated as a result. It was their last hesitation. The stillness was shattered by the roar of eight instruments of death of various calibers fired almost at once. Collins collapsed from five slugs and crumpled into a lifeless lump between the two horses. Simpson screamed as a bullet tore off his left ear, then screamed no more as three more lethal pieces of lead tore into his chest. He jerked backward, then slumped over the saddle horn in the peaceful slumber of death. A half dozen bullets knocked Bradley out of the saddle. His right foot caught in the stirrup as he fell to the ground. Bradley's mount let out an awful animal shriek as a bullet tore into its neck. The terrible din ceased as suddenly as it had begun. Captain Billie surveyed the bloody scene there on the ground before him. He holstered his pistol and sighed.

"Somebody kill that hurt horse," he said.

Blue Steele hesitated at the river bridge. He had a thought that stopped him. Silently he reprimanded himself for a fool. He had been concentrating his thoughts and his inquiries on local folks. That was okay so far as it went, he thought. It probably was someone local who was behind the killings. That was the only way to make any sensible connection between the two incidents, and Steele felt certain that some connection existed. But he himself had said that the shootings had a professional look about them. That probably meant that the killer was someone from outside—a stranger to the communities. If his original thought was correct, and he still believed that it was, then someone local had hired a professional assassin to perform the unpleasant tasks for him. He was getting nowhere with his line of questioning into the local possibilities—who might want to kill both Luton and Fields. Perhaps the other approach would lead somewhere. Who actually did the shootings? If he could answer that question, the answer might just lead to the one who had done the hiring, the one with the motive, the local one. He jerked the reins to turn his horse around and ride back into Riddle's main street. There were two hotels to check. At the Riddle Hotel the desk clerk said that business had been slow. He had his regular residents but had not had any transients for a while. At the Riverside he found where

Oliver Colfax had spent the night. The date was well after those of the shootings, and Miller had told Steele about Colfax's strange appearance in town. The hotel register of the Riverside simply confirmed what Miller had said.

Yet Colfax was a known professional killer, and Steele was suspicious of the man. He was looking for such a man, and this one had come to town asking questions about the Luton shooting. Steele did not believe in coincidence.

"Had you ever seen Colfax in here before that day?" he asked the clerk.

"Don't believe so. Don't know as how I ever seen the man before."

"And you haven't seen him since?"

"Nope."

Steele stopped back by Miller's Emporium to inform Miller of his new line of inquiry and to ask the acting marshal if he knew of the presence of any strangers in town anywhere around the dates of the shootings. The answer he received was negative. Steele rode on across the bridge and stopped at Jack's House.

"Hello, Blue," said Jack as Steele stepped into the saloon.

"Jack, have you had any strangers through here lately?"

"No. Mostly just the regulars. Same ones in here nearly every night. Only Stan Bragg don't come in since Fields got killed."

"I mean, hotel guests."

"Oh. Well, not many. There was a drummer through here a couple days ago. Up from Omaha. Selling farm implements."

"Anyone else?"

"No. Not just lately. Let's see. Yeah, there was one guy. It's been a while back, though. I never did hear his line of work. I would have took him for a gambler, but he never came in here to play."

"What was his name?" said Steele.

"Cherry," said Jack. "Funny name, ain't it? That's how come I remember it."

"First name?"

"Can't recall. You want me to check the register?"

"Yeah, Jack," said Steele. "This could be important."

Jack moved out from behind the bar and led the way into an adjacent room that served as the hotel lobby. He walked around to the other side of the counter and pulled out the register.

"Here it is," he said. "Leiland. Leiland Cherry."

"Let me see that," said Steele.

Jack turned the book around so that Steele could read it.

"He was here the night of June thirtieth," said Steele. "That right? Just the one night?"

"Yeah. Just like it says. But he was here once before. I'd say about a month earlier—maybe more. Here."

He turned the book back around and flipped some pages.

"Here it is," he said. "Just one night that time, too. Eighteenth of May."

He's the man, said Steele to himself. It's got to be him. The dates are right.

"Jack, what's this Cherry look like?"

"Aw, Blue," said Jack, scratching at his cheek, "how do you say what a fella looks like? He dressed slick. You know, like a businessman or a gambler, something like that. Black three-piece suit. Tie. Derby hat, I think. Yeah. Little derby."

"Was he a big man?"

"No, Blue, I wouldn't call him big. About your size, I'd say. Sort of medium, I guess."

"How old a man is he?"

"Damm it. Now how would I know that?"

"Well, would you say he was fifty?"

"Not that old."

"Twenty?"

"No, he was older. Thirty, maybe."

"What color hair?"

"Hell, I don't know. He had on his hat whenever I saw him."

"Dark eyes?"

"No. Real light blue. Almost no color. You know what I mean? Real kind of washed-out or something. Weird-looking. And blond hair. Yeah. So blond, it was almost white."

Steele slapped Jack on the shoulder.

"Thanks," he said. "Anything else comes back to you about this Cherry, you let me know. Okay?"

Back in his office, Steele wrote down all the information on Leiland Cherry he had gotten from Jack. Then he opened a desk drawer and pulled out a stack of wanted posters. He went through the stack of dodgers carefully, but he found no Leiland Cherry, and no pictures of anyone under any name that fit the description given by Jack.

Damn, he thought. If Sarge was here, he'd likely know all about the man.

Emily pulled back on the reins to stop the horse, then set the brake on the buggy. She looked at George Fisher, who stared at her, not moving. She saw Ryan at the door to the shack, holding Matt there before him. She wondered where Colfax might be.

"Mom?" said Matt.

She cringed at the fear in her son's voice, at the plea, the questioning. She had to protect him, to get safely away from these men.

"Are you all right?" she said, and she heard a quavering in her own voice.

"Yeah," said Matt. "I guess so."

For the first time George Fisher moved, but only ever so slightly. He turned his head just a bit to snap at Matt over his shoulder.

"Shut up," he said, then he faced Emily again directly. His lips twisted slowly into a contemptuous smirk. "Come on down, darling. I've got a surprise for you inside."

Emily could well imagine what kind of surprise George Fisher had in store for her. Visions of his past brutality flashed through her mind. She recalled the pain and humiliation and the constant fear. She looked again at Matt and read the terror in his young face. Then her right hand came out from under the folds of her wide skirt, and it held the Smith and Wesson pocket .38—the one Ryan had dropped in the lobby of the Cross Timbers—and she raised it up and pointed it at George Fisher. Fisher opened his mount as if to speak, but the roar of the .38 came first. The slug tore into Fisher's chest. A puzzled, stupid expression overcame his face as he looked down toward the pain and the red splotch on his shirtfront. His knees turned rubbery and he collapsed. Ryan started to pull Matt back into the shack just as Colfax stepped out into the open.

"Hold it right there, mister," he said.

Matt broke loose from Ryan's grip and ran to his mother, who clutched him to her desperately.

"Don't shoot," said Ryan. "I'm not armed. I lost my gun."

"He's got a knife, though," said Matt.

"Let's see it," said Colfax.

"Yeah. Sure. Don't shoot."

Ryan reached carefully inside his coat with his left hand and produced the weapon.

"Here it is," he said.

He held it out gingerly by a thumb and one finger at arm's length before him.

"Drop it," said Colfax.

Ryan did as he had been told, and Colfax walked on down to the buggy. He glanced at Emily and Matt.

"Are you two all right?" he said.

"Yes," said Emily. "I think so."

"Your father and the sheriff will be along shortly. You just relax if you can. I need to have a talk with this man."

Chapter Fourteen

In the distance Colfax could see two riders approaching, moving fast. That would be Hal Decker bringing the sheriff. Colfax figured that he had no time to waste. He wanted information from this man, and he might have to beat it out of him. If the man had killed Luton for his boss, Colfax would have to kill him. He had sworn it. He didn't want the sheriff around to witness how that would take place. He took a deliberate aim at Ryan, as if he intended to execute him then and there. Ryan dropped to his knees in the hot dust.

"Don't," he said. "Please."

"Talk to me," said Colfax. "It might keep you alive longer."

"What? What do you want me to say?"

"What brought you and your boss to Texas?"

Ryan pointed a trembling finger at Emily and Matt, who were seated together in the buggy.

"Them," he said. "Mr. Fisher wanted to get them. He wanted to take them back to Boston. That's all. He made me come along."

"Why now?" said Colfax. "Why after all these years?"

"He sent me after them once before," said Ryan, "but I didn't get them."

"Sarge Luton tossed you off the train," said Colfax.

"I didn't know who he was. I went back to Boston, and Mr. Fisher fired me."

"Then he hired you back? How come?"

"He sent for me a while after that. I went to his office, and he had been beat up pretty bad. He asked me to describe the man that had tossed me off the train. I did, and he said it sounded like the same man. He'd come all the way to Boston. Mr. Fisher never said, but I guessed that it was to warn him away from Miz Fisher, there. He gave me my job back, and he never said anything more about coming after them—until this time."

Colfax looked toward the approaching riders. They were getting close.

"Go on," he said.

"Well, just recently I was reading in *The Police Gazette,* and I saw his picture in there. The man who had thrown me off the train. It was Luton. The story said he'd been killed. I took it to Mr. Fisher, and he sent me right out to get train tickets for both of us."

"A damned coward," said Colfax, "and you were his dog. I ought to kill you right here."

"I told you everything," said Ryan. "Don't shoot."

"You told me a good story. How do I know that Fisher didn't find out where Luton was and send you to kill him?"

"I told the truth. We never knew who the man was. Not until I found that story. It's the truth."

Colfax eased the hammer down on his revolver and holstered the weapon. Decker and the sheriff were within hollering distance, and he thought that Ryan was probably telling it straight. He would let the sheriff have Ryan. Without his boss the man would be no threat to Emily and Matt, and he would almost certainly spend a long time in a Texas prison for kidnapping. If Colfax was guessing wrong, he could always go after Ryan again.

He stepped over to the buggy and saw the .38 where Emily had dropped it between her feet.

"Excuse me, ma'am," he said, and he picked up the pocket pistol and tossed it in the dirt beside the body of George Fisher.

He was conscious of light on the other side of his eyelids. It was not much consciousness, but it was all he had. Then a vague but persistent question began insinuating itself into that small area of awareness attempting to expand it. There must be a source of that light. There must be something out there in that light. The light must be coming from somewhere, from something. Some thing. Out there. Out where? To the consciousness behind the eyelids it must have been like the moment of creation, or at least like the first glimmer of awareness to new life forming in a womb. *I am aware, but who or what am I, and of what am I aware?* Consciousness, awareness without knowledge.

Slowly, gradually, but with physical certainty, other sensations invaded his limited field of perception: pain, vague and dull and general; and a gnawing, deep down hunger. The gnawing hunger from the depths of his being developed into a desire. He wanted food. His consciousness was growing by the second with new sensations, new desires, new knowledge. His eyelids lifted, slowly, to flood his brain with an unbearable flash of light. Quickly he clamped them back shut. He squeezed them tight, trying to shut out the pain. Gradually they relaxed again, but he wanted the light. He allowed them to open once more, slowly, but with more control, just a little. He could feel them twitch in protest against the brightness. The twitches became blinks, letting the light through in pulsating flashes. Then the adjustment was made, and he stared out at his strange surroundings.

As his eyes adjusted to the light and his consciousness began to feel vaguely familiar, he realized that he was not a stranger to the room in which he found himself. He had seen it before. When? Where was he? He didn't know. He couldn't call it back to his memory. The questions became more urgent, and he tried to remember something—anything. What was the last thing he could recall? The last thing before this—? Nothing came to his mind except pain. The thinking, the trying to recall hurt. Then the hunger overcame his consciousness again.

Hal Decker dismounted before his horse had come to a halt, and he ran to the buggy.

"Are you two all right?"

He clutched both Emily and Matt in one large embrace.

"We're fine, Daddy," said Emily.

Red Squiers dismounted and stepped over to the body of George Fisher. He looked at the .38 there in the dirt beside the remains, picked it up, tucked it into his waistband, then glanced at Colfax.

"It seems pretty obvious to me what happened here," he said. Then he pulled a set of handcuffs out of a rear pocket and moved toward Ryan, who was still kneeling on the ground.

"Get up," he said. Ryan stood up, and Squiers turned him around by his shoulders, then secured his hands behind his back with the cuffs.

"How'd you two get out here?" he said.

"Mr. Fisher paid a man in town to drive us out," said Ryan.

"Red," said Decker, "I'll take Emily and Matt back into town in the buggy. You can put him on the horse I rode out."

"Okay," said Squiers, "but I ought to make him walk."

Decker climbed into the buggy, but before he could whip up the horse, Colfax stepped over to stop him.

"Emily," he said, "I've got to go on up into Indian Territory. I've got another lead to follow up there. Maybe I can take you out to the Milam ranch like I promised when I get back. I don't want to let this go any longer."

"It's all right," said Emily. "You'll let me know?"

"Yes."

"Colfax," said Decker, "thanks for all your help."

He flicked the reins and the buggy started with a lurch. Colfax turned to Squiers.

"Sheriff," he said, "you want to make this rat walk part of the way back?"

Squiers gave him a quizzical look.

"I left my horse down the trail a ways last night."

"Oh," said Squiers. "Hell, yes. You climb on that one and lead the way."

"Thanks," said Colfax. He strolled over to the horse Decker had left.

"You, Boston," said the sheriff. "Start walking—that way."

Ryan looked out in the direction in which the sheriff was pointing—the general direction of Henrietta. He could see nothing but slightly rolling prairie. He glanced at the body of his boss, George Fisher, the man who had brought him to this state, and he spat. Then he sighed deeply and mournfully, and he began to walk.

Colfax was back on the M. K. & T. Railroad, popularly known as the Katy. It would get him into the Choctaw Nation much more quickly than could a horse, and he was beginning to feel neglectful of his self-assigned duties. He had followed a trail to Texas— the trail of Bradley and Simpson—only to be delayed by the intrusion of George Fisher. True, he had considered for a brief while the possibility that George Fisher might be the culprit he was after; and that slight possibility, along with the need he felt to protect Emily and Matt, had made the digression worth his while. Strange, he mused, to allow himself to be momentarily distracted by a sense of need to protect someone other than himself. That had never happened before in his life, and the realization of that fact brought with it a peculiar tickling sensation to some obscure part of his brain. He wondered about the source of this new motive in his life.

Of course, he thought. Emily had been Luton's woman. He had gone to her defense because of Luton—and because George Fisher might have been responsible for Luton's murder. But then he admitted to himself that he had never really believed Fisher to be guilty of that crime. In his mind it had been only a slight possibility. His sights had been set on Bradley and Simpson almost from the beginning. So he had moved his sights for a short time for the sake of Emily and her kid. But the biggest surprise of all to Oliver Colfax was that this discovery of a new motive for action in his life produced in him an equally new and rather pleasant sense of self-satisfaction and—yes—self-worth. *My God,* he thought, *I found that one good man, and he's invaded my*—the next word came slow, hard—*my soul.*

Hal Decker climbed down out of the buggy and then helped Emily to dismount while Matt jumped out the other side. Will Milam was slowly walking from the house to join them. No one spoke as Emily stepped toward the lonely-looking mound of earth. She did not weep, but her father and her son both noticed the tightening in her jaws. When Milam arrived, Emily spoke to him without looking in his direction.

"No marker?" she said.

"I—uh—didn't think he'd of wanted one, ma'am."

"He's been out here all this time," she said. "I didn't know. With your permission, Mr. Milam, as this is your property, I'll obtain a marker—and I'll bring some flowers."

Milam cleared his throat and shuffled his feet nervously, stirring up puffs of hot dust.

"I'd of told you," he said, "but I never knew it would of meant anything to you."

"They were going to get married," said Decker.

"Oh, my God," said Milam. He turned and walked a few steps away, rubbing his forehead. Then he turned back to face them. "I—uh—I think we need to have a talk," he said. "Would you all come into the house with me?"

All three visitors to the grave looked at Milam with curious expressions. None responded to his question.

"Please?"

"The name on the hotel register is Leiland Cherry," said Steele. "I got this description from Jack."

He handed a piece of paper across the table to Miller, then picked up his coffee cup to take a sip. For once he had managed to catch Miller alone and get him out of his store. They sat at a booth in a café around the corner from Miller's Emporium. Miller read through the notes on the paper, then looked up at Steele.

"I never saw the man," said Steele, "but when you put this description—clothes and guns—with the man's cautious behavior and the dates of his stays at Jack's House, it sure makes me suspicious."

"But where do we look for this man?" said Miller. "We don't even know if this is his right name, do we?"

"I don't know where to look, and hell no, we don't know. But I think this—whoever he is—is our killer. I think he's a professional killer, and I think someone hired him to kill Sarge and Lance Fields."

"But why?"

Steele took another sip of coffee.

"I don't know," he said. "I don't know. What we have to do is keep trying to figure out why anyone would want to kill either Sarge or Fields and then try to find a connection between the two."

Miller waved a hand at the waiter, who came to the table with a coffeepot and refilled the cups. When the waiter had retreated once again to what Miller thought was a sufficient distance, he spoke again.

"I've never seen anyone around here who looks like this," he said, jabbing a finger at the description on the paper.

"Neither have I, Mr. Miller," said Steele, "and I can't find anyone who has, except for Jack. The man got his room and went to it. Paid in advance. Jack never saw him again. Same thing both times. I went through all the handbills in my office and couldn't find his name or a description that matches his on any of them."

"Well," said Miller, "it's probably a long shot, but let's look in Sarge's office. See if we find anything there."

The front door of the café opened, and Doc Gallager rushed in.

He looked hurriedly around the room, spotted Miller, and quickly stepped over to the table.

"C. J.," he said, "we got to talk."

"Sit down, Doc," said Miller.

"No. I need to see you alone. Sorry, Steele."

"It's okay," said Steele, starting to get up. "You can sit here."

"No," said Gallager, "you finish your coffee. C. J., step outside with me for a minute, will you?"

"Excuse me, Blue," said Miller.

Through the café window Steel could see the other two men in animated conversation. A few minutes passed, and he finished his coffee. Once he noticed Miller glance in his direction. The waiter came by to offer more coffee, but he refused it and paid up. Then Miller and Gallager came back inside.

"Blue," said Miller, "let's go on down to Sarge's office. We've got something to tell you, and we need privacy for it."

He turned to Doc Gallager.

"Doc," he said, "you go get Rudy and Clarence and bring them along to the office. They ought to be in on this."

Chapter Fifteen

Will Milam paced the floor of his living room. He had seated his three guests and served them each a large glass of lemonade. He, himself, drank whiskey. He was trying to find the right words, a task that never came easy to Milam, except when he was issuing orders to the rough cowhands who worked his ranch. Finally he faced Emily, but he did not look at her. He looked at the floor. He drained his whiskey glass before he spoke.

"It's been eight years," he said.

"I know," said Emily.

"Yeah. Of course you do. But it's been eight years, and even back then, he never said nothing to me. If I'da had any idea, I'da told you right away."

"Any idea of what?" said Emily.

"You and Sarge. I didn't know."

"I didn't, either, eight years ago, Mr. Milam. He only recently wrote me to propose marriage. I really don't know what you're getting at."

"You said you'da told," said Decker. "Told what?"

Milam went for his bottle and poured himself another whiskey.

"That grave out there," he said. "They's a empty box in it. That's all. It ain't a real grave."

"What?" said Decker.

"You heard me right. He ain't out there."

"Well, where is he?" blurted Matt.

"Far as I know," said Milam, "he's still up in Riddle, Ioway. Far as I know, he's still alive."

"You know where Sarge kept his dodgers?" asked Blue Steele.

"There's time enough for that," said Miller. "We've got something to tell you."

"A kind of secret to let you in on," added Clarence Dry.

Dry and Miller looked at Doc Gallager, who gave a slow nod in agreement. The three conspirators wore long and guilty expressions on their faces.

"All right," said Steele. "I'm listening."

"Blue," said Miller, "Sarge is alive."

Blue Steele looked at Miller, who found himself unable to return the Indian's hard gaze. He fastened his eyes on Steele's shirtfront. Steele was seated in the marshal's chair behind Sergeant Bluff Luton's tidy desk. Slowly he leaned back and placed his feet on the desktop. He crossed his arms over his chest.

"Tell me the whole story," he said, "and by God, it had better be good."

Oliver Colfax stepped off the train in Tuskahoma, the capital city of the Choctaw Nation. It was not his first visit to the Choctaw Nation, yet he was still a bit amazed at the typicality of the small city. Except for the abundance of dark faces visible on the streets, Colfax thought that he might as well be in any small American city west of the Mississippi River. A few of the Indian men wore blankets folded over their shoulders, but even these were dressed, under the blankets, like the average white man. Colfax stepped toward a Choctaw citizen on the sidewalk.

"Excuse me, sir," he said.

The Choctaw responded in words that Colfax could not understand—the Choctaw language, he assumed. Another Indian man, apparently noticing the dilemma, approached the attempted conversation.

"Can I help?" he said.

"Thanks," said Colfax. "I hope so. I'm looking for the headquarters of the Lighthorse."

The man pointed diagonally across the street to a two-story building constructed of red stone.

"They're in the capitol building," he said, "on the first floor."

"Thank you."

Colfax tipped his hat to both men, turned, and walked to the capitol building. He noted the look of stability as he walked up to the front steps, and for the first time he realized that he was, in fact, in a foreign land. This was a national capitol building. The Choctaw Nation was a nation unto itself—separate from the United States. He opened the heavy front door and stepped inside. He was met almost immediately by a young Indian in a three-piece suit and tie who asked his business and then escorted him to an office down the hall. Colfax thanked the young man and stepped inside the office. From behind a large desk, Captain Billie looked up. His face registered recognition.

"Ah, Mr. Colfax, isn't it? When I last saw you, you weren't feeling well."

"Oh," he said, "yeah. You're—uh—"

"Captain Billie of the Choctaw Lighthorse."

The policeman stood and held out his hand for Colfax, who took note of the limp handshake of the Indian.

"You and your friend," said Billie, "had just very nearly wiped out a gang of train robbers. The one you failed to kill, we captured."

"Yeah."

"But one of them had knocked you on the head—probably the one we caught later. And your friend—what was his name? Luton. Yes. Mr. Luton had ridden away on one of the outlaws' horses. I never got to thank him."

"Yeah," said Colfax. "That's more or less the way I remember it."

Captain Billie motioned toward a chair, and Colfax sat down. Billie leaned back in the chair behind his desk.

"Where would your version differ from mine?" he asked.

"Captain Billie," said Colfax, removing his hat and placing it upside down on the floor beside his chair, "I'm going to tell you the truth—the whole story. I'm going to do that because I want your help."

The policeman settled back in his chair and interlaced his fingers behind his head.

"All right," he said.

"A little over eight years ago," said Colfax, "just a little while before we met, I was hired to kill Sarge Luton. That was how I made my living in those days."

Captain Billie raised his eyebrows slightly, but otherwise his expression remained unchanged. Colfax continued his tale.

"I always told my victims of my intentions, and I always waited before killing them until I had convinced myself that they deserved it. I also always managed to provoke a fair fight, if you get my drift. That way I could avoid thinking of myself as a murderer.

"I could live with my profession, Captain, because of a firm belief in the total depravity of man. In a way I was like that old Greek searching for one good man."

"Diogenes," said Captain Billie.

Colfax looked up, caught off-guard by the interruption.

"You surprised that an Indian knows about Greek mythology, Mr. Colfax? We have a thorough curriculum in our National Seminary."

"We live and learn," said Colfax, shaking his head slowly, "and the older I get, the more ignorant I find out I am. I found that good man."

"Mr. Luton."

"Yeah. I couldn't kill him. Didn't want to. I grew to like him. Well, he went his way and I went mine. I had to abandon my profession. Or maybe I should say, alter it somewhat. I've done some bounty hunting, but even then I tried to bring them in alive.

"It was while I was stalking Sarge and after I'd told him my intentions that the train robbers hit. You got the story all right, except for one thing. It was Sarge who hit me."

Captain Billie smiled.

"I had my suspicions," he said. "What is it you want from me?"

"Sarge was murdered recently, Captain. I want to find the man who did it."

"And kill him."

"Yes."

"I'm sure you recognize the irony in your situation, Mr. Colfax."

"Yeah."

"Why did you come to me?"

"Down in Texas eight years ago, Sarge spoiled a pretty setup for some gun slicks. There are only two of them left. Their names are Bradley and Simpson. I was told that they were up here in your country. The only other suspect I have is that train robber who got away, but you just said you caught him."

"We did. He served his time, got out, and went back to his chosen profession. This is an interesting coincidence, Mr. Colfax. Brad Collins, your train robber, joined forces with Bradley and Simpson, the very men you're looking for."

Colfax leaned forward in his chair expectantly.

"Do you know where they are?" he said.

"All dead, I'm afraid."

"Damn."

"Killed attempting to rob a train at Perryville."

Colfax stood up and paced the floor in angry frustration.

"Dammit," he said. "Goddammit. A dead end. That was my last lead. Now how the hell will I ever know?"

Captain Billie watched Colfax pace back and forth for a moment or two before he spoke.

"Maybe I can help," he said.

Colfax turned on him almost viciously.

"How?" he said.

"Do you know when Mr. Luton was killed?"

Colfax reached into an inside coat pocket and jerked out the crumpled copy of *The Police Gazette*, turned and folded the proper page. He gave it a quick glance.

"May nineteenth," he said.

"May nineteenth. Bradley, Simpson, and Collins have been here since sometime before that, Mr. Colfax. I've had my eyes on them the whole time. They've not been out of the Choctaw Nation. They couldn't have done it."

Colfax put a hand to his forehead and thought hard for a moment.

"Thank you," he said. "Thanks. I've got to start all over again."

"Where will you go?" said Captain Billie.

"Back to Iowa," said Colfax. "That's the only place now. Riddle, Iowa."

Chapter Sixteen

Will Milam opened a drawer in his desk and withdrew a folded sheet of paper. Slowly, like a tired old man, he crossed the room to Emily.

"This here came with the box," he said. "I never read it. Can't read. I had to get my foreman, Curly, to read it to me, so he knows, too. Nobody else knows."

He handed the paper to her, and she unfolded it carefully, as if she were afraid of breaking it. She read it through silently.

"What's it say?" said Decker.

Emily's hand was visibly shaking as she started back at the beginning of the letter, this time reading aloud.

"It's dated May twentieth," she said "From Riddle, Iowa.

Dear Mr. Milam,

I am writing to you as a friend of Bluff Luton, our town marshal here in Riddle, to ask your help for his sake. Sarge has been shot. At first we thought he had been killed, and the word spread quickly that he had been. But he is not dead, just very nearly so. We have taken him to Doc Gallager's place for care and recuperation, but as we have no law now and a killer loose amongst us, Doc and I decided not to correct the initial story that got out. If the killer knew that he had failed, he would probably try again. So we enlisted the aid of Clarence Dry, undertaker, and he has become part of our little conspiracy. Clarence said that we should pretend to ship the body out of town for burial to avoid questions about a funeral, an open casket, a hasty burial, etc. So now you are the fourth party involved, if you will agree, as I hope you will for his sake. The casket we sent you is sealed and contains only sandbags. Please bury it as if it were the real thing, and please tell no one the truth. Bluff Luton's life may depend on this deception. In the meantime we will try to determine the identity of the would-be assassin and pray for the quick and complete recovery of our good friend. I wouldn't involve you in this except that you are the only friend of his that I know of outside of our town. Thank you for your help.

Sincerely,

Coleman J. Miller
Mayor
Riddle, Iowa

Emily sat staring at the letter. Hal Decker stood up and walked to her side. He put a hand on her shoulder and with his other hand took the letter from his daughter to read it again for himself. Matt had also sprung up from his seat and moved to his mother's side.

"Mom," he said, "he's alive."

"That there letter's the only word I've got from up there," said Milam. "It says he was bad shot. We don't know if he's alive or dead."

Emily stood up and straightened her dress. She was obviously ready to leave Milam's house.

"Dad," she said, "I've got to go to him."

"Yeah, honey, I know," said Decker. "We'll put you on the next train."

"Me, too?" asked Matt.

"Yes," said Emily. "We'll both go."

"Why the hell didn't you tell me in the first place?" said Steele.

"We agreed to keep it between just the three of us," said Miller. "A secret's a hard enough thing to keep as it is. The more people in on it, the harder it gets."

"You didn't trust me."

"It wasn't that, Blue. It was just—well, what I said. We didn't consciously exclude you. We just decided to keep the secret. Once we'd made the decision, we stuck by it."

Steele stood up and stalked to the door of the office. He opened the door and stood looking out into the street. Dark clouds were rolling in from somewhere over Nebraska, moving slowly and ominously toward Riddle.

"Looks like rain," he said.

"Could be," said Clarence Dry in a nervous voice.

"You know," said Steele, "if you three jackasses were across the river in my jurisdiction right now, I'd lock you up for obstruction of justice."

"Now just a minute, Steele," said Gallager. "We haven't obstructed anything."

"Sarge might know something that would help straighten this whole damn mess out," said Steele.

"Sarge has been unconscious ever since we found him shot," said the Doc. "It's been uncertain whether he'd live or die up until just now. As soon as I saw a change, as soon as he showed signs of coming around, I told C. J., and we decided then and there to tell you."

Steele turned back into the room to face the other three men.

"All right," he said. "All right. Forget it. Where is he?"

"In my office."

"I want to talk to him."

"Not just yet. He's still too weak. He's not out of danger yet."

Steele expelled an exasperated sigh, then walked up close to Gallager.

"You let me know as soon as I can talk to him. You let me know right away," he said.

"I will," said the Doc.

"Even before you go running to these two," said Steele, "you tell me. You got that? Now, Mr. Miller, where do you suppose Sarge has stashed those dodgers?"

"'Samson said to them, "Since you would do a thing like this, I will surely take revenge on you, and after that, I will cease." So he attacked them hip and thigh with a great slaughter.' And how many of us, my friends, like Samson of old, have sought revenge on those who have done us wrong? And if not in actual physical aggression, at least in our hearts and minds? Have you felt the desire for revenge? Have you? Of course you have. I have. We all have. And why have we? Because we are weak. Because we are mere humans. Because we are abject sinners, my dear friends.

"Samson was wrong to take revenge, and we are wrong when we seek revenge, or even desire it. If someone has wronged us, on earth there is the law, and on earth it is the right and duty and obligation of the law to set that wrong to right again. 'Then Paul, looking earnestly at the council, said, "Men and brethren, I have lived in all conscience before God until this day." And the high priest Ananias commanded those who stood by him to strike him on the mouth. Then Paul said to him, "God will strike you, you whitewashed wall! For you sit to judge me according to the law, and do you command me to be struck contrary to the law?"

"'Beloved, do not avenge yourselves, but rather give place to wrath; for it is written, "Vengeance is Mine, I will repay," says the Lord.'

"It is not our place to seek vengeance, my friends and neighbors. It is not given over to us. On earth, in this life, it is the task of the law of the land. But there is a higher law, and there is a higher authority, and it is unto that Almighty that we must ultimately appeal for justice. Has someone done you wrong? Spurned you? Scorned you? Stolen from you? Smitten you? Yea, even taken the life of one you loved? Do not say, like Samson, 'Since you would do a thing like this, I will surely take revenge on you.' No. Do not. Rather, pray to God on High as in *Jeremiah*.

"'But, O Lord of hosts,
You who judge righteously,
Testing the mind and the heart,
Let me see Your vengeance on them,
For to You I have revealed my cause.

"'But, O Lord of hosts,
You who test the righteous,
And see the mind and heart,
Let me see Your vengeance on them;
For I have pleaded my cause before You.

"'For we know Him who said, "Vengeance is Mine, I will repay," says the Lord. And again, "The Lord will judge His people."' And if we ask Him, He will hear, and 'I tell you that He will avenge them speedily.'"

Reverend Flagle stood just outside the front door of the church at the top of the stairs so that none could escape the clasp of his clammy palm when making an exit. He was sweating profusely, having just given himself over completely to his passion for his favorite sermon. He had just vigorously pumped the hand of Victor Bragg. His next victim was young Stanley Bragg, sheepishly following in his father's footsteps. His mother was right behind him. Flagle grabbed Stanley's right hand in his and did his best, it seemed, to crunch its bones. He dropped his large left hand heavily on Stanley's right shoulder and gave it a hearty squeeze.

"Ah," he roared, "the prodigal son has returned. The lost lamb is back in the fold. We haven't seen you here for a long while, young man."

Stanley stared at the reverend's paunch to avoid looking him in the eyes.

"No, Reverend," he said. "I guess not."

"Ah, well, welcome back. Follow the Lord and stray no more. Stay on the straight and narrow. God rejoices in your return, Stanley, as do I."

"Yes, sir. Thank you."

Mrs. Bragg beamed with pride as she stepped up for her turn to shake Flagle's hand. Then the Braggs descended the steps together. They were met in the street by Coleman J. Miller.

"C. J.," said Victor Bragg, "how are you this morning?"

"Just fine, Victor. Mrs. Bragg. Stanley. Good to see all of you here at church together. Looks like rain."

"Probably by nightfall," said Mrs. Bragg.

"We were just going over to the Frontier Place for lunch," said Victor Bragg. "Would you care to join us?"

"Thanks," said Miller. "I will."

When lunch was finished and Miller reached into his pocket for his wallet, Victor Bragg caught his wrist and held it.

"No, no, C. J.," he said. "This is on me."

"Victor—"

"I insist," said Bragg. "Please."

Miller relaxed his arm and Bragg released it.

"Thank you, Victor," said Miller. "It was a good meal, and I enjoyed the company. I get a little tired of eating alone all the time."

"Well," said Mrs. Bragg, "we'll have to do this more often."

Outside, Miller stood for a moment on the sidewalk watching the Braggs walk together down the street. It was nice to see the family together. Mrs. Bragg seemed happier than he could remember having seen her look for some time, and old Bragg himself was actually pleasant. It was nice, but something about it puzzled Miller, and he couldn't quite give utterance to it.

Blue Steele had made a list of all the law officers in the cities and towns surrounding Riddle, Iowa, and West Riddle, Nebraska. Then he composed a telegraph message:

IF YOU SEE LEILAND CHERRY OR OLIVER COLFAX HEADED MY WAY, PLEASE INFORM ME AT ONCE. ALSO, ANY INFORMATION YOU HAVE ON CHERRY WOULD HELP ME.

He folded up the list and the message and tucked the papers into a pocket. As West Riddle had no telegraph office, he would have to ride across the bridge to send the message. He still had no information at all concerning the mysterious Leiland Cherry, if that was even the man's right name. But he knew that Oliver Colfax was a professional killer, and he suspected that Cherry was the same. It was the only line of investigation open to him.

As Oliver Colfax rode the Katy north, his head swam with a myriad of disjointed thoughts. He recalled his first meeting with Bluff Luton, remembered his announcement to Luton of his intention to kill him, relived the final battle with Luton which he had won, but which, he admitted only to himself, he had won with luck. It easily could have gone the other way. He thought about all the little things he had noticed about Luton—how the man had dealt with women and children, how he had dealt with Colfax, his announced assassin. Colfax recalled with somber reflection his old philosophy and reflected on how Luton had blasted it for him, had forced him to revise his opinion of humankind and alter his chosen profession.

His thoughts also focused in on Luton himself, Luton the man, Luton the good man. He painfully considered that he had liked Luton, that he . . . missed the man. He had discovered at long last a man he could admire, a man he respected, liked, could have been friends with, and someone had killed the man. Someone—who? Colfax gritted his teeth in frustrated anger. He wanted to know. Who had killed Luton? And why? Why would anyone kill such a man? The irony of that question surfaced in his mind, and he chuckled at himself, at his own momentary lapse into naïveté.

Whatever the reason, he wanted to know who had done it, and he wanted to kill that man. Oliver Colfax, the professional killer, had never before in his life wanted to kill a particular human being. It had always been just business, but this one, whoever it was, he wanted to kill. This particular murderer had deprived the world of a good man, had deprived Colfax of a—what? Of a friend? Colfax had not seen Luton in eight years, had not tried to see Luton. He would not because of a feeling that the town marshal wouldn't want to be associated with a known killer. For Luton's own sake, Colfax had stayed away. Yet he considered Luton a friend, even though he had determined to keep his distance by a self-imposed exile from that friend.

And he, himself, Colfax realized, was not the only individual the murderer had deprived by means of this killing. There were Emily and her son, Matt. They had just been given a chance at a new life—a new life with a fine man—and it had been taken from them before it had begun. Why, Colfax wondered all of a sudden, had Luton waited eight years to propose to Emily? Eight long years. He thought of the man as he had come to know him. Luton must have considered marriage to Emily eight years ago. He must have. He had gone well beyond the demands of the chivalric code to protect her, having made a special trip to Boston to warn George Fisher to stay away. Then he had simply returned to his job in Riddle and kept to himself for eight long years.

Of course, Colfax thought, Sarge would not have considered himself worthy of the lady. In fact, he decided, the real question was not why he had waited eight years, but how he had finally convinced himself, gotten the courage, to ask her at all. That was the real question. He mentally shrugged it off. There was no way he would be able to answer that one, and after all, he decided, the years fly by once one has reached his forties. Perhaps the eight years hadn't seemed like such a long time to Luton. Perhaps they had passed him by before he had realized it. He forced his thoughts back onto the trail of the killer.

It had not been Bradley and Simpson, had not been Collins, had not even been George Fisher. He had no other suspects, no more trails to follow. He would have to look for a fresh trail in Riddle. Once back in Riddle, he would talk to that mayor again, that— Miller was his name. In Riddle, they thought that Luton had no enemies. Well, he had at least one, and there must be a clue somewhere. Colfax was damned determined to find it.

Chapter Seventeen

Sam Andersen jumped at the first sounds of the message coming through. It had been a slow and quiet day, and he had just about dozed off in his chair. He grabbed his pencil and pad and wrote furiously until the clicking had ceased. Then he tore the top page off the pad, ran to the door, and opened it. Out in the street, ten-year-old Joshua Dobbs was riding his bicycle. It was the only bicycle in Riddle, and Joshua was proud of his uniqueness, his freedom, and his speed. Sam waved at him and hollered.

"Josh," he said. "Come here."

Josh wheeled the bicycle around and headed over toward the sidewalk where Sam stood. He slammed on his brakes, skidding and throwing up dust clouds.

"What?" he said.

"You know where the marshal's office is over in West Riddle?"

"Yeah. I ride over there all the time. I know where everything is."

"You know Marshal Steele?"

"The Indian?"

"That's him. Listen, I got a telegraph message for him. You take it over to him for me and I'll give you a nickel. Okay?"

Joshua put the nickel in his pocket, the paper under his cap, and headed for the bridge. At the end of the street he made a hard left turn. The rear wheel almost went out from under him, but he managed to keep the machine upright. Then he stood up on the pedals to get more power behind his strokes. When he hit the bridge, he wanted to fly. He knew it could be done. He had managed it before. He pumped the pedals as if the fate of the nation depended on the message under his cap getting to the Indian marshal on time, and for all he knew, it did. Then he hit the bridge. The bicycle didn't exactly fly. It hopped. But both wheels were off the ground at the same time for just an instant. When it came down on the bridge, it jarred Joshua clear up into his brain. The cycle wobbled a bit. He righted it. Then he settled down to steady, serious pedaling and clattered on across the Missouri River bridge into West Riddle, Nebraska.

Blue Steele was walking from Jack's House back toward his office when Joshua Dobbs came racing down the main street of town and shrieking in his high voice.

"Marshal. Marshal."

Steele turned to face the desperate youngster just as Josh hit his brakes and slid to a stop, almost falling over sideways.

"What is it, boy?" said Steele. "Jesse James coming?"

"No, sir," said Joshua, taking off his cap and producing the paper. "Important message from across the river. Mr. Andersen sent me. Paid me a nickel, too."

Steele took the note and read it.

"This is important, boy," he said. "What's your name?"

"Joshua Dobbs, sir."

"Well, Josh," said Steele, "I think you've earned more than a nickel. Here."

He pulled a coin from his pocket and handed it to Josh.

"Gee," said Josh. "This is a dime."

"Yes, sir. Thanks for bringing the word, Josh. You did a good job."

"Thank you, Marshal," said Josh as he shoved the dime into his pocket. He turned his bicycle around and headed back toward home. Steele went to get his horse.

Emily had thought that she'd stay on the train. The stop at Tuskahoma was to be a short one, and she had no taste for sight-seeing. But Matt was restless.

"Can I get off for a while?" he asked. "I'll be okay, and I'll be back in plenty of time."

"All right," said Emily. "I'll go with you."

"You don't have to get off if you don't want to."

"Oh, it'll probably do me good to have a short walk, anyway."

They left the train and began walking along the main street in the Choctaw Nation's small capital city. Indians were everywhere.

"Mom, look," said Matt.

"What?"

"Across the street. It's one of those Indian policemen. See?"

Captain Billie was walking briskly along on the opposite sidewalk. Emily was surprised that she recognized the man from eight years ago.

"I remember the uniforms," said Matt. "I was only seven, but I remember those guys. You think he's one of the same ones we saw before?"

"Indeed he is, Matt," said Emily. "He was the one in charge. Come on. Let's talk to him."

Emily looked up and down the street to check the traffic, then led Matt diagonally across at an angle calculated to intercept the policeman, but the tactic failed. As they neared the other sidewalk, Captain Billie was on ahead. Emily thought quickly, and the name came back into her mind.

"Excuse me," she called from behind him. "Captain Billie."

Billie stopped and turned to see who it was hailing him on the street, and Emily and Matt hurried on up to him.

"Excuse me," said Emily. "You probably won't remember us. I'm Emily Fisher and this is my son, Matt. When you last saw us, he was much smaller."

"As a matter of fact," said the policeman, "I do remember you. I wouldn't have recognized the young man, though." He turned toward Matt. "You have grown some since then."

"Yes, sir," said Matt. "I guess I have."

"This is interesting. Eight years ago we met because of a train robbery—the three of us and Mr. Colfax. I never saw Mr. Luton, but I heard about him. The robbers were all killed by Mr. Luton and Mr. Colfax, except for the leader, Brad Collins, who was sent to prison. Eight years passed, and I didn't see any of you again until just recently, when all of a sudden I've seen Collins and Colfax and now you two."

"You've seen Collins?" said Emily.

"We killed him the other day while he was attempting another train robbery," said Captain Billie.

"Oh. And Mr. Colfax?"

"Yes. I've seen him, too. Do you have time to sit down over a cup of coffee?"

Emily glanced toward the train where it rested beside the depot.

"Yes," she said. "I think so."

"Come with me."

Captain Billie led Emily and Matt into a small café and got them a table. He ordered coffee for himself and Emily, and a bottle of ginger beer for Matt.

"Mr. Colfax came to see me," he said. "He was looking for three men: Brad Collins and two men named Bradley and Simpson. They were the ones we killed during the robbery attempt."

"He thought that they might have killed Bluff Luton, didn't he?" said Emily.

"Yes, but they couldn't have done it. They were all up here at the time of the murder."

"Captain Billie," said Emily, "Mr. Luton is not dead. The story about his having been killed was false. He was shot and apparently very badly hurt. We're on our way now to see him."

Captain Billie thoughtfully rubbed his chin for a moment. He expelled a murmuring sigh.

"I hope," he said, "that someone tells Mr. Colfax before he commits a murder."

"Yes," said Emily. "I hope so."

"You may find him in Iowa," said the captain. "That's where he was going when he left here."

"Then I probably will see him up there."

"Mom," said Matt, "we'd better go."

Emily opened her purse to get out some change.

"Please," said Captain Billie, "allow me."

"Thank you," she said, "and thank you for the information. I wish we didn't have to rush so. Good-bye."

Will Milam sat alone drinking whiskey. He had spent the day out working with his crew. That had kept his mind off things. But the day's work was done, and he was alone. He didn't socialize with the cowboys who worked for him. He felt too old for their company. Even Curly Wade, his foreman, the most mature, sensible, and dependable of the bunch, seemed to Milam not much more than a boy. He drained his whiskey glass and then carefully refilled it. He wondered if Bluff Luton were alive or dead. *Damn him*, he thought, *if he'da come in with me way back whenever I asked him to—either time—none of this wouldn't never have happened.* He wondered whether or not Colfax would manage to find the assassin—or would-be assassin—who had shot Luton. *Damn. I hope so. I hope he kills the son of a bitch dead.* But in an afterthought he told himself that he hoped that Colfax didn't kill the bastard too quickly. Make him suffer.

Milam felt guilty somehow. It didn't make any sense to him, yet he had the feeling. He felt like maybe he should have been more persuasive in offering Luton half his ranch. But, more to the point, because it was more recent, he felt guilty for having helped put Emily through what she had been made to suffer. Of course, Milam had been unaware of any romance between Luton and Emily, but that didn't help how he was feeling. He figured that

Colfax and Emily and Matt were all on their way to Riddle, Iowa, and he wondered for a moment if maybe he shouldn't head up that way, too, to find out for himself just what the hell was going on. Then he poured himself another whiskey and sipped it.

Colfax was tired. It crept into his mind that he was getting old, but he stubbornly refused to acknowledge the thought, fought off giving it words. But he was tired. Too much time on the road—train rides, horseback, more train rides, then the stagecoach for the last leg on into Riddle. It was a rough-riding old son of a bitch, too, the stage. He was anxious to put more questions to Riddle's mayor, but he figured that would probably have to wait. He thought that he would get a room first. Then he'd get a bath and get some sleep in a good bed. The morning would be time enough for the questions.

When the stage pulled into Riddle, Colfax was its only passenger. He was up from the seat and reaching for the door even while the stage was still rocking back and forth from its stop. He groaned from sore, stiff muscles as he stepped down onto the street, and he felt the jar of his connection with solid ground drive upward through his bones.

"Oliver Colfax?"

Colfax looked up, and there before him, holding shotguns, were Miller and two other men. He did not recognize the other two.

"Mayor," said Colfax, "what's the meaning of this?"

"Put your hands up over your head, Mr. Colfax" came another voice—this one from behind him. Colfax looked slowly over his shoulder. There was a fourth man also armed with a shotgun—an Indian by his looks. Colfax raised his hands. The man standing to Miller's right stepped forward and pulled the Colt from its holster high on Colfax's belt. Then he stepped quickly back.

"Walk straight ahead," came the Indian's voice.

The four men marched Colfax to the marshal's office and locked him in a cell. Then they put their shotguns in a cabinet on the wall. Two of them left. Miller and the Indian stayed. Colfax noticed a badge on the Indian's vest.

"All right," he said, "you've got me behind bars. Can you tell me now what this is all about?"

"Mr. Colfax," said Miller, "this is Blue Steele, town marshal from across the river. He's working with us while we're temporarily without our own town marshal."

"Why have you locked me up?"

"Someone shot our marshal," said Miller.

"Hell, I know that. I talked to you about it. You know that I'm looking for the killer myself."

"I know what you said, Colfax. I don't know if you told me the truth."

Steele walked over to the cell.

"Colfax," he said, "we have reason to believe that the shooting was done by a professional killer. You are a known hired assassin, and soon after the incident you show up in Riddle asking questions about it. Wouldn't you say that looks just a bit suspicious?"

"I didn't kill Sarge," said Colfax.

"Nobody did," said Steele. "He's not dead."

"What?"

"You heard me right," said Steele. "Most of us were kept in the dark about that for a good while. He was shot, all right, but it didn't kill him."

"You mean to tell me," Colfax said, looking at Miller, "that there is no killer, and yet you knowingly allowed me to ride out of this town with murder in my brain? I had three suspects down in the Choctaw Nation. I might have killed them."

"Why didn't you?" asked Steele.

"The law did it before I got there. I slowed down in Texas to help a lady out of a jam."

"That doesn't sound like you, Colfax," said Steele, "judging from your reputation."

"She was Sarge Luton's fiancée. Do you people have any idea of the torment you have put that lady through? She thinks he's dead."

"We didn't know that Sarge had a fiancée," said Miller.

"We still don't," said Steele, eyeing Colfax with suspicion.

The mayor moved around behind Luton's desk and opened a drawer.

"Wait a minute. There was a letter from Texas," he said. "Here it is."

He removed the letter from the drawer and studied the envelope. Steele stepped over to stand beside him.

"What was the lady's name?" said Steele.

"Emily," said Colfax. "Mrs. Emily Fisher."

"Mrs.?" said Miller.

"She's a widow," said Colfax, and he pictured in his mind the crumpled body of George Fisher lying in the Texas dust.

Steele and Miller exchanged a glance. The return address on the envelope showed the same name Colfax had just given. Miller spoke to Steele in a low voice, almost a whisper.

"Should we open it?" he said.

"No," said Steele. "Not yet. If he's telling us the truth, Sarge ought to be the first one, the only one, to read this letter. We'll give it some more time."

"Well," said Colfax impatiently, "am I right?"

"You got the name right," said Steele. "All that proves is that you know some things about Sarge and this case that we don't know."

"You just told me that Sarge is alive. Obviously there is no killer. I didn't kill him. Let me out of here."

"You didn't kill Sarge," said Steele. "That's true enough. But there is a killer. A young man named Lance Fields was murdered across the river. Same style as how Sarge was shot."

Frustrated, Colfax turned away from the conversation. He ran a hand through his hair and stalked the floor of the cell like a caged and angry badger. Suddenly he turned back on the other two men.

"You've got nothing to hold me on but your own ill-founded suspicions," he said. "If you tried to take me to court on this, a judge would throw it out."

"You're not charged with anything," said Steele, "and we can hold you on suspicion."

"For a while," added Miller.

"Where's Sarge? Go get him. Ask him. He'll tell you I didn't do it."

"Sarge is in no condition to be bothered with questions," said Miller. "We said he's alive. We didn't say he's well."

Colfax sighed and dropped onto the cot that stood against one wall of the small cell. Trying to talk to these two, he thought, was like trying to talk to dried mule droppings. The irony of his situation was compounded, and even in his frustration, in a small corner of his mind, he found it all just a bit amusing. He had originally planned to kill Luton for money, had decided against it, then someone else had attempted to kill Luton. Thinking Luton dead, Colfax had set out to find the murderer and kill him, and finally Colfax was locked up in Riddle, Iowa, as a major suspect in the shooting. *They'll probably hang me for it*, he thought. Then another thought came creeping to the front of his mind. Something Steele had said had nudged it to life from some secret niche or gulley. He stood up and walked to the bars.

"You said a .44-40 in the back?"

"That's right," said Steele.

"Same thing across the river? .44-40 in the back?"

"Yeah. Why?"

"Several reasons, Marshal. First off, I don't own a .44-40. Never have. In the second place, I don't work that way. If you know so much about my reputation, you ought to know that. Third, I haven't hired out like that in eight years. If you kept abreast of the things important to your profession, you'd know that, too."

"Is that it?" said Steele.

"Almost."

"Well?"

"I know a man who does work like that."

Chapter Eighteen

Bluff Luton opened his eyes. He had been awake before in this room. This time he was not so puzzled as before by his surroundings—or by the question of his own identity. He felt pain, he was weak, and he was tormented by a ravenous hunger gnawing at him from the depths of his guts. But he was more fully conscious than he had been the time before, and he had questions. He wondered how he had come to be in this room, in this bed. He thought back, trying to bring to mind any events that might explain his situation. He remembered a fuzzy awakening. There had to be something back beyond that. He strained to recall. He remembered first a sense of frustration, an uneasy feeling of indecisiveness and—yes—inadequacy. And the source of that feeling had been what? The letter. Of course. He had been writing a letter. He had written it. And he had mailed it. And he had wondered about it. And worried over it. What would be her reaction? Emily.

My God, he thought, *how long have I been here like this? Has she answered my letter? My—proposal? What must she be think-*

ing? With a sudden sense of desperation Luton tried to raise himself from the bed, but a sharp pain went stabbing through his back and into his chest.

"Ah."

He shouted and fell back again onto the pillow. The room became black again, but only for an instant. Strangely shaped lights danced before his eyes as he drew in deep, fast breaths. The door opened, and a figure, obscured by the flashes, rushed into his view.

"Bluff. You awake?"

Recognition slowly came to Luton as he squinted at the intruder.

"Doc?" he said.

"Yeah. It's me. How do you feel?"

"I'm hungry as hell, Doc."

"Good," said Gallager. "That's good. I'll have Irma fix you up a good broth."

"Broth? I could eat a mule, Doc."

"Yeah, I know, but we have to start easy. Do you have much pain?"

"Well, yeah, but I can stand it. I feel as weak as a puppy, Doc."

"It's going to take some time for you to get your strength back. Now that we can start getting some nourishment into your body, that'll help."

"Doc?"

Gallager waited a few seconds for Luton to continue, but Luton was silent, seemingly lost in thought.

"What, Bluff?"

"What happened?"

"Someone back-shot you. Just as you stepped out of your office. It appears to have been a long rifle shot—from a .44-40. We came close to losing you. In fact, we thought that you'd been killed for just a short while. Now, you just take it easy. I'll go order up that broth for you."

Gallager turned to leave the room, but Luton stopped him at the door with a question.

"Wait, Doc. This is important. Can you find out if I got any mail?"

"Bluff," said the doc, "you just try to relax. I can't have you worrying about things while you're trying to heal."

"It's important, Doc. I'll worry until I find out."

"All right. I'll check. Now, you take it easy. Irma will be along soon."

Gallager left the room and shut the door. Luton stared after him for a moment, then slowly rolled his head back to stare at the ceiling. The anticipation of something to eat—even broth—made his hunger seem even more intense. He began to feel impatient. Where was Irma with his broth? How long would it take Gallager to return with his mail? If he had any mail. Had she answered his letter? And if she had, what had she said?

C. J. Miller looked up from behind his counter when he heard the bell over the front door jingling to signal the entrance of a customer. Ruth Bragg walked in jauntily.

"Good day, Mr. Miller," she said.

"Hello, Mrs. Bragg."

Miller took note of her cheeriness and remarked to himself at the change in spirits she seemed to have undergone just recently. It must be because her son had resumed attending church with the family on Sundays, he thought. Something had caused Stanley's behavior to change, and that, in turn, had brought about this change in Ruth. It was curious, but Miller was pleased to see the woman feeling good these days.

"What can I do for you?" he asked her.

"I want to get Stanley a new Sunday suit," she said. "Something real nice."

"Well, all right," said Miller. "I think I've got just the thing. Right over this way."

He led the way to a rack of suits and removed one to show Mrs. Bragg.

"How do you like this one? Nice brown three-piece. Conservative cut. Fine workmanship. Take a look at this lining. See? Of course, we'll alter the length of the trousers."

She fondled the material of the coat while she thought. Then she stepped back and cocked her head to one side.

"I'm not so sure about the color, Mr. Miller," she said. "I think maybe black is more appropriate for Sunday, don't you?"

"I've got a black one just like this," said Miller. "Here."

He placed aside the brown suit and selected a black one.

"This more like it?" he said, holding the suit up for her inspection.

"Yes," she said, "I like that one."

"What about the size? This looks about right to me, but you can't always tell by looking."

"I'm not exactly sure, Mr. Miller."

"Well, I tell you what. Why don't you ask Stan to stop by here after he gets off work? Is he working at the bank today?"

"Oh, yes. He's at work now every day, and he's at home each evening and to church with us on Sundays."

"Well, just have him stop by and try it on. I'll need to measure him to get the trouser length, anyway."

"Will it be ready by Sunday?"

"I think so."

"All right," said Mrs. Bragg. "I'll stop by the bank before I go home."

"Fine," said Miller. "You want me to just put this on the bill?"

"That will be fine, Mr. Miller. Thank you so much."

As Ruth Bragg left the emporium, C. J. Miller watched after her for a moment. Something was bothering him about all the sudden changes in the Bragg family. *But they're all obviously much happier now than before,* he told himself. *Why should I worry over it? I should be happy for them.* He tried to push the thought out of his mind by taking the black suit over to the counter and writing a note to attach to it, but he found himself still wondering about the Braggs. *Of course, I should have thought of it sooner. Stanley got the shock of his life when Lance Fields was killed right beside him. It changed him. Put the fear back in him and sent him back to church. It's a natural reaction. With Stanley back in the fold, his parents, especially his mother, are much more content. Sure, that's the whole explanation.* As he folded the suit and tucked it under the counter, the bell over his door sounded again, and Doc Gallager came hurrying in.

"Hello, Doc," said Miller.

"C. J.," said Gallager when he had reached the counter, "he's conscious. He's awake."

"Sarge?"

"Who else? Yes, Sarge. I just sent Irma to take him some broth."

"Well, how is he, Doc?"

"At this point I think he's going to pull through just fine."

"That's great, Doc. Just great. You know, Blue Steele wants to question Sarge. Should we—?"

"No. Not yet. Absolutely not. I don't want him bothered with all that until he's got a little more strength back. Another day or two, maybe."

"Okay, Doc. You're the boss. But if Sarge can help us find this killer, we sure do need to talk with him."

"I know that, and I'll let you and Steele know just as soon as I can. Oh, listen, C. J., Sarge is real agitated over his mail. Do you know anything about it? I seem to remember Kirby bringing you a letter once in here."

"It's over in Sarge's office, Doc."

"Can we get it? I promised him I'd check on it for him."

"I can't leave the store right now," said Miller, "but I've got the key to the marshal's office. I'll get it for you."

Blue Steele arrived at the Riddle marshal's office and jail just as Doc Gallager was unlocking the front door. He rode up to the hitch rail, dismounted, and wrapped the reins of his horse once around the rail.

"Morning, Doc," he said.

"Hello, Steele."

"I was going over to the emporium to get Mr. Miller to open this up for me," said Steele. "You saved me the trouble."

"Yeah? Well, I guess it's okay."

Gallager walked on in, and Steele followed. Inside the cell, Colfax raised his head up from the cot to see who had come in. Gallager walked around behind the desk and opened up a drawer. He found the letter he was looking for and removed it.

"What are you doing, Doc?" asked Steele.

"C. J.'s okayed this," said Gallager defensively.

"That's Sarge's letter you got there."

"Yes."

"Why?"

Gallager paused before answering Steele. Then he straightened himself up, gave Steele a defiant look, and spoke. "I'm taking it to him," he said. "That's why."

"Is Sarge conscious?" asked Steele.

"Yes. But I don't want you or anybody else talking to him. Not just yet. I didn't even want him reading his mail, but he insisted. To keep him quiet, I agreed. Like I told you before, I'll let you know when you can talk to him. Now get out of my way."

Steele stepped aside and Gallager left the office. Colfax stood up from the cot and walked over to the bars.

"You go talk to Sarge," he said. "He'll tell you to let me out of here."

"Colfax," said Steele, "if you'll talk to me, you might get out. Who the hell is the killer you know who shoots from behind with a .44-40?"

"Let me out of this damned cell and I'll talk to you. Not before. Why should I help you? I don't want the man arrested anyhow. I mean to kill him."

Steele paced the floor, then he walked around behind Luton's desk and sat down in the chair, propping his feet up on the desktop. He stroked his chin thoughtfully, staring at Colfax.

"Is the man's name Cherry?" he asked.

Colfax looked sideways and squinted at Steele. Then he gave a slight shrug of his shoulders.

"How'd you figure that out?" he said.

"A man stayed at the hotel across the river at the right times to have done both shootings. He signed the register with the name Leiland Cherry. I got a description from the hotel. Slight build. Blond hair. Blue eyes. Smart dresser."

"That's Lee," said Colfax. "He did it, then. He's our man. Goddammit, Steele, why don't you let me out of here?"

Doc Gallager opened the door to the bedroom and walked in carrying the letter. Luton tried to raise himself up from the bed. He groaned and fell back.

"Just you lay still," said Gallager. "I've got your letter here. How are you feeling?"

"Better, Doc, thanks. That little bit of broth did help, but I'm still hungry."

"We'll feed you a little more after a while. Here."

Gallager handed Luton the letter, and Luton glanced quickly at the envelope, then ripped it open and started to read.

"I'll be damned," he said.

"What is it?" said Gallager.

Luton finished reading the letter, then he started to read through it again.

"Sarge," said Gallager. "What is it?"

Luton lowered the letter, letting it rest on his stomach. He looked at the doc, an amazed expression on his face. Then he smiled.

"She said yes, Doc. By God, she said yes."

Chapter Nineteen

Oliver Colfax had been stuck in the Riddle jail for just about twenty-four hours. He alternately paced the floor in extreme agitation and stretched out on the cot for periods of apparent tranquil resignation to his unhappy situation. Throughout this routine he thought and planned. He wanted out. Of course, he would have wanted out of a jail cell under any circumstances, but he had a job to do, and he wanted to get on with it. The news that Sarge was alive had been more than welcome, and he realized that had he originally heard that Luton had been shot but not killed, he probably would not have embarked on this trek. But the hunt was in progress, and he could not bring himself to abandon it. It had become like any other job, and Colfax always finished his jobs. That compulsion had once driven him, even after he had realized that he would not kill the man, had no desire to kill him, had, in fact, grown to like him, to force a fight to the finish with Bluff Luton. The drama had ended when Colfax, holding his Colt on the downed lawman, had turned the barrel and fired into the ground.

So Sarge was alive, but the fact remained that someone had attempted to murder him and very nearly had succeeded, and that someone was almost without a doubt, Lee Cherry. Colfax knew Cherry. He had never liked the man, but his dislike had nothing to do with his craving to kill. He had never killed for such a reason. He had killed for money and to defend himself, and now he planned to kill for revenge. No, he thought, not revenge—justice. Killing Lee Cherry would be justice. The man had shot Sarge Luton—a good man. He wanted out of the jail so he could pursue Cherry. He knew that he could find Cherry. And he would kill him. One way or another, he would get the job done.

Colfax was up and pacing the floor. He heard through the open barred windows of his cell the clatter of the stagecoach rolling into Riddle, and he stepped over to the window to watch. Any distraction in his unpleasant and nearly intolerably boring confinement was worthwhile. The coach passed by his window, and he thought with frustration of his arrival by the coach exactly one day previous to this one. The dust from the horses' hooves and the rolling wheels rose to fill the air and floated through the window into the cell.

Colfax squinted his eyes against its attack but continued to watch as the driver hauled back on the reins on down the street, and the coach rocked to a halt. The driver set the brake and climbed down from the stage box as the dust settled in the street, and the passenger door within Colfax's view swung open. A young man dressed neatly for traveling stepped out, then turned as if to help someone else follow him.

Colfax had a sense of recognition, but not until the lady followed was it fully realized. He clutched bars with both hands and pressed his face between them to shout, "Emily! Matt!"

The two disembarked passengers turned their heads in confused surprise.

He shouted again and thrust an arm through the bars as far as he could, to wave at them. "Down here, Emily. It's Colfax."

Matt spotted the arm waving through the window and ran toward it, his mother following at a more dignified pace. When

138

Matt reached the window and saw the face of Colfax through the bars, he was the first to speak.

"Mr. Colfax," he said, "why are you in jail?"

Colfax waited until Emily had stepped up beside her son to answer the question.

"My reputation preceded me here," he said. "They locked me up because they think that I might have shot Sarge."

"But that's ridiculous," said Emily.

"Listen," said Colfax. "He's alive."

"I know," said Emily. "That's why we're here. Mr. Milam told us."

"So he was in on it, too," said Colfax. "Sure. He'd have to be. The grave is on his land. I've been played for a fool from Texas to Iowa."

"Mr. Colfax," said Emily, "we've got to find Mr. Luton. He'll tell them to let you out."

"You can't see him. There was a lawman in here yesterday arguing with the doctor about that. Apparently, Sarge has improved, but the doc still doesn't want him bothered by visitors."

"Surely he'll let me see him."

"Maybe. Go find a man named Miller. He's the mayor here, and he owns a store just down the street called Miller's Emporium. Maybe he'll talk to the doc for you, and maybe you can help me convince him to let me out of here."

"Miller's Emporium?" said Emily.

"Right."

"We'll be back," said Matt. "Don't worry. We'll get you out."

C. J. Miller took Emily and Matt directly to Doc Gallager's place.

"Doc," he said, "this is Mrs. Emily Fisher and her son, Matt."

"Sarge's fiancée," said Gallager.

"Yes," said Emily. "Please let me see him."

"All right, but just you. Sorry, son. Let me go in first and tell him. I want to avoid any sudden shock."

"Of course, Doctor," said Emily. "I understand."

Gallager left the room.

"Mom," said Matt, "I'll go and take care of our bags, and then I'll wait for you at the jail with Mr. Colfax."

"All right, Matt."

"You know Colfax?" said Miller.

"Yes, indeed, Mr. Miller," said Emily. "He's been a great help and comfort to us through all this. I think you're doing him a disservice by holding him in jail. He can't be guilty of this shooting."

"Perhaps you're right, Mrs. Fisher. I don't know, but I'll go along with your son, if that's all right."

"Thank you."

Gallager returned, and Miller and Matt excused themselves and left.

"Mrs. Fisher," said Gallager, "right this way."

Emily stepped into the room as Doc Gallager pulled the door quietly shut behind her. She stood there, just inside the door, for a few seconds. There in the room, lying in bed before her, wide-awake, his face wearing an expression that she could only interpret as love, was the man she had so recently thought she would never see again. The man she had thought to be dead.

"Oh, Bluff," she said.

"Emily."

She walked over to stand beside him and took his hand in hers. She felt tears welling up inside her eyes, but she managed to hold them back.

"How do you feel?" she said.

"Seeing you here, I feel much better. Right now I'm sure glad that I wrote that letter."

"I am, too," said Emily, "but why did you wait so long?"

"I was afraid of what you'd think," he said, "of what you'd say. I don't know how I finally got up the courage to go ahead and

140

write and to take a chance on making a fool out of myself. All I can think of—all I remember going through my mind—is just that I had developed a kind of restlessness. I felt like there was something I ought to be doing that I wasn't doing—that something was missing from my life. I guess I realized finally that it was you, and I decided that it was worth the risk of showing myself a fool."

"Bluff, the only foolish thing you did was wait so long."

"I'm just glad that it wasn't too late."

"What counts now is what's ahead of us. I love you, Bluff."

Emily leaned over the bed and kissed him gently on the forehead.

"I love you," she said again, "and Matt admires you so much. He needs someone to be a father to him."

"I'll do the best I can," said Luton, "for both of you."

You'll do just fine."

"Well, maybe, if I can just get myself up out of this bed and make myself useful again."

"You stay right where you are until your doctor says that you can move. Do you hear me? When you do get up, I want you whole and healthy and strong. Matt and I will be here."

He looked at her and smiled at the stern expression on her face. It was an expression that said she cared for him, that she was deeply concerned, and it was an expression that said she had entered his life and assumed a certain amount of control, and he liked it.

"All right," he said. "I'll do as you say. With you here now, I can afford to be a little more patient than usual. Where is Matt?"

"The doctor wouldn't let him come in with me to see you," said Emily, "but he's here. He came with me. He wouldn't have it any other way. Mr. Miller took him over to your jail to see Mr. Colfax."

"Not Oliver Colfax?"

"Why, yes. Oh, Bluff, I wasn't thinking. So much has happened since—well, during the time you've been laid up here. They seem to think that Mr. Colfax might have shot you."

"That's crazy," said Luton. "If Colfax had wanted to kill me, he could have done it eight years ago. Besides that, back-shooting is not his style. What's he doing here, anyway?"

"He's been trying to find out who shot you. He thought you were dead, and he intends to kill the man who did it."

"Hunh."

Luton smiled. He recalled the day eight years ago, the last time he had seen Oliver Colfax. He had been lying on the ground in a north Texas mesquite thicket. Colfax had been standing before him, his Colt aimed at Luton's chest. Then Colfax had moved the six-gun, fired it into the ground beside Luton, said, "It's finished," mounted his horse, and ridden away. Luton had not seen Oliver Colfax again. Yet somehow he was not surprised to find out that the man was searching for his assailant.

"Emily," he said, "would you ask the doc to come in?"

Emily opened the door and called out to Doc Gallager, who came immediately into the room.

"What is it?" he said.

"Doc," said Luton, "where are the clothes I was wearing when I was brought in here?"

"I've got them," said Gallager, a look of suspicion on his face.

"And all the stuff that was in the pockets?"

"Yeah."

"Would you please locate my house key and give it to Emily for me? Then go with her down to my office and tell C. J. Miller I said to let Oliver Colfax out of jail. Right now. And apologize to him. Then one of you take Emily and Matt over to my house. They'll be staying there."

"I'll do all that on one condition," said Gallager.

"What's that?"

"Just as soon as we walk out of here, you settle yourself back down and get some rest."

Luton looked at Emily, then back at Gallager.

"I promise," he said.

"C. J.," said Doc Gallager, bursting through the door into the marshal's office, "Sarge says to let Colfax out right now—with an apology."

Emily walked into the room right after Gallager, and Matt quickly stepped over to stand by her side.

"The apology won't be necessary, gentlemen," said Colfax. "Just open the door."

"I said we'd get you out of here," said Matt, his face beaming with pride.

C. J. Miller's face, however, had changed hue slightly as he'd moved to the desk to get the keys.

"Well," he said, "if Sarge says so, I'll do it. And I am sorry for any mix-up, Mr. Colfax."

He unlocked the cell door and opened it wide, then went back to the desk. Colfax followed. Miller opened a drawer and dropped the key ring back in. He shut that drawer and opened another from which he brought out Colfax's gun belt and holster. He handed the rig across the desk to Colfax, who strapped it on high around his waist, the holster holding the big Colt around front and toward the center. He turned to face Matt and Emily.

"Thank you," he said. "Are you two situated all right?"

"We have the key to Bluff's house," said Emily. "We're all right. Thank you for your concern."

Colfax touched the brim of his hat and gave a slight nod.

"Then I'll be seeing you," he said, and he headed for the door.

"Mr. Colfax," said Miller.

Colfax turned and looked at Miller, and there was no friendliness in his expression.

"Mr. Colfax, may I ask what your intentions are now? Where are you going from here?"

"I'm going where I meant to go when you met me upon my arrival in your town, Mr. Miller. I'm going to get a room in the hotel and have myself a bath."

When Colfax had walked out and shut the door behind him, Miller got up from the chair behind the desk and started for the door.

"Now where the hell are you going?" said Gallager.

"I'm going across the river to see Blue Steele."

Miller left without saying another word. Doc Gallager looked awkwardly around himself. Then he looked at Emily.

"Well," he said, "that just leaves us. We might as well go, too. Come along, and I'll take you to Sarge's house."

Colfax had taken his bath and dressed in fresh clothes. He was strapping his Colt back on when he heard a knock on his door.

"Who is it?" he said.

"It's C. J. Miller."

"Come in, Mr. Miller. The door's unlocked."

Miller stepped in. He had an uneasy look about him. He held his hat in both hands just about at the level of his solar plexus, and he was fidgeting with its brim.

"Mr. Colfax," he said, "I've just come from Blue Steele's office across the river. He's down in Sarge's office now, waiting for me to come back. And you. We'd like to meet with you about this business. Doc Gallager will be there, too. He's on our Town Council."

"Why me?" said Colfax.

"Well, we're all interested in the same thing. We want to catch this murderer."

"No, you want to catch a murderer. I don't give a damn about that killing across the river. I want to kill the man who shot Sarge Luton."

"It's the same man."

"Probably."

"It won't take up much of your time to come to our meeting," said Miller.

"Why should I want to meet with you folks, Miller? You threw me in jail. I already know what my intentions are."

"What are your intentions?"

"I told you. I mean to find Lee Cherry and kill him."

Miller fidgeted with his hat brim some more.

"But maybe we can all work together," he said.

"I don't need you."

Miller gave a slight shrug of his shoulders and turned to leave the hotel room. His back to Colfax, he hesitated, then he turned around again.

"And that'll be the end of it?" he asked.

"Yes."

"This Leiland Cherry," said Miller, "he's a professional killer, isn't he?"

"That's right."

"Then someone paid him to kill Sarge. That man, whoever he is, is as guilty as Cherry. Maybe more. And we don't even know who he is."

Colfax stared hard at Miller for a brief moment.

"Whoever he is, if he really wants Sarge dead, he might try again. So what if you kill Cherry? He'll just hire someone else. Or maybe even try it himself."

Colfax still didn't respond.

"Do you know who the man is? Will Cherry tell you?"

Colfax knew Leiland Cherry. He knew also that Cherry would never tell him or anyone else the name of the man who had hired him for a job—not under any circumstances. The task of killing Cherry was going to be difficult at best. Cherry was good. Trying to get any information out of the man in the process would be futile. He knew that. And Miller was right, Colfax admitted to himself. Cherry had shot Sarge with no emotion and for no reason other than to collect his fee. It was the other man, the unknown, who was the real guilty party. And he probably would try again with another hired killer if necessary, just as soon as he found out that Sarge was still alive.

"I'll meet with you, Miller," he said.

They gathered in Bluff Luton's office: Colfax, Miller, and Blue Steele. Doc Gallager was the last one to appear, and he came in the office hurrying and slightly out of breath. All wore stern faces.

"Before anyone says anything else," said Gallager, "I've just talked to Sarge. C. J. he wants you, in your capacity as mayor and acting marshal, to make Colfax a deputy."

"I'm not interested in being a lawman," said Colfax.

"That's what Sarge said you'd say," Gallager snapped back. "He also said to tell you that it's temporary, it's without pay, and that it's what he wants. He said you'd do it for him."

"All right," said Colfax. "I'll go along."

"That's settled, then," said Miller. "Now we have to make some plans. How do we go about this business? What's our next step?"

"We have two problems," said Blue Steele. "We have to get Cherry, and we have to find out who hired him and get that man."

"Are you any closer to finding out who did the hiring?" asked Gallager.

"No," said Steele. "We haven't come up with anyone who had a reason for killing Sarge—or Lance Fields."

"What about your theory that the killer might have hit Fields by mistake?" asked Miller. "That he might have been aiming for young Bragg?"

"Even there," said Steele, "I haven't found anyone with a reason for killing Stan."

"Forget that," said Colfax. "Lee Cherry doesn't make mistakes."

"And Colfax says that Cherry will never talk," said Miller, "so even if we could get him alive, here, under arrest, we'd be no further along on that question than we are right now."

"There's other angles," said Colfax, and the others all turned to him, waiting for him to continue.

After a brief pause Steele spoke up. "What are you thinking about, Colfax?" he said.

"Men like Lee Cherry don't work cheap. Who around here has more money than he knows what to do with? Make a list. Then who on that list might have gained something from killing Sarge—or that other fellow?"

146

"Mr. Miller," said Steele, "can you and Doctor Gallager, here, take care of that?"

Miller shot Gallager a quick look and nodded his head.

"Yes," he said, "we'll get right at it."

"The other thing is," said Colfax, "to correct your first story about Sarge. Let it out that Sarge is not dead. That will bring Lee Cherry back to town. I know. He won't leave a job undone. It's a matter of . . . professional pride. It might even flush the other one out in the open—the man who hired him. Might."

"But won't that put Sarge in danger?" asked Miller.

"Yeah," said Colfax. "I reckon it will. But it's up to us to keep him protected."

Miller and Gallager looked inquisitively at Blue Steele.

"He's right," said Steele. "It sounds to me like it ought to work. At least it's doing something. I'm for it."

"I'd suggest," said Colfax, "that you even exaggerate the situation a bit. Say that Sarge is not only alive, but well and back at work. I'll change my clothes for some of his, make a habit of sitting in this office, keep my hat—his hat—pulled down low. Maybe I'll sucker Cherry right in here. Put a couple of guards—good men—on Sarge around the clock, just in case."

"And I'll hang out across the street," said Steele. "Try to keep you covered and watch out for who comes into town."

Colfax nodded in agreement.

"Are we all agreed, then?" said Miller. "Then let's set it in motion."

Chapter Twenty

Leiland Cherry smoothed back his long, greasy blond hair and eyed himself in the mirror. He cocked his head from one side to the other, slicked back a stray strand he found, then, satisfied, picked up his suit coat and put it on. He took up his derby from the table that stood beside the door of the Omaha, Nebraska, hotel room he called home, placed it on his head, stepped out into the hallway, and carefully locked his door. He walked to the end of the hall and down the stairs. As he passed by the front desk in the hotel lobby, the morning desk clerk looked up.

"Good morning, Mr. Cherry," he said.

Cherry perfunctorily touched the brim of his derby and kept moving. He did not deign to speak to the clerk. He walked outside and stopped on the sidewalk. Hands on hips, he looked up and studied the sky. Clouds were moving in from the west. Then he looked both ways up and down the street before crossing it to go inside the restaurant that was directly across from his hotel. He went inside and took a seat at a table just inside the door and by the front window. The waiter was by his side in a matter of seconds. Cherry was a creature of habit when he was at home, and when he was at home, those people he dealt with catered to his habits.

"The usual, Mr. Cherry?" asked the waiter.

Cherry nodded. As the waiter hustled off, Cherry removed his derby and placed it on the chair next to the one he sat on. The waiter returned quickly, with a cup of coffee and a bowl of sugar cubes in his hands and a folded newspaper under his arm. He placed the coffee cup on the table in front of Cherry, the bowl in the center of the table, and the newspaper to Cherry's right. Then he hustled off again. Cherry put four lumps of sugar from the bowl into his coffee and stirred it. Then he sipped from the cup. Satisfied with the flavor, he set the cup back on the saucer and picked up the paper.

Cherry was reading on page three when the waiter returned with his breakfast: two poached eggs and one slice of dry toast. He had also brought the coffeepot, from which he refilled Cherry's cup. Cherry spread the paper out on the table, off to the left of his plate. He put four lumps of sugar into his newly refilled cup and stirred it. He sipped from the cup and replaced it on the saucer. Then he picked up one poached egg in a spoon and took it in one bite. He followed that with a bite of dry toast and another sip of coffee. Then he glanced again at the paper, and a headline toward the bottom of the page caught his attention.

REPORT OF MARSHAL'S DEATH PROVES FALSE

Cherry leaned over the page to read the story.

Sergeant Bluff Luton, popular town marshal of Riddle, Iowa, was recently mistakenly reported to have been killed in Riddle by an unknown assassin. Luton was shot in the back on the evening of the nineteenth of May this year. Rumors of his death spread quickly and reached the press, to be widely reported before the truth was discovered.

Luton has recovered from his gunshot wound and is reportedly back at work. There are as yet no suspects in the May nineteenth shooting incident.

Cherry tore the story from the page and tucked it into a pocket of his vest. He removed his wallet, took out a bill, and carelessly flipped it onto the table, then got up and left the restaurant. His second cup of sweetened coffee, second egg, and the remainder of his dry toast were abandoned, and the waiter was pleasantly surprised at the size of his tip from Leiland Cherry that morning.

The guests all began arriving at Doc Gallager's at about the same time. All were dressed as if for church. Blue Steele and Maribel were there, and C. J. Miller and Clarence Dry. Oliver Colfax stood to one side of the room with Matt Fisher.

Miller walked over to Doc Gallager.

"It's about time, isn't it?" he said.

"Yeah," said Gallager. "I shouldn't even have allowed this, but Sarge insisted. It's got to be now, he said."

"Is he dressed and out of bed?"

"Yes. He's all duded up and sitting in a chair. He says he'll stand up when the time comes."

"Where is Reverend Flagle?" said Miller, pulling the watch out of his pocket and studying it. "It isn't like him to be late."

"Damned if I know," said Gallager.

"I don't see why we couldn't have gone," said Ruth Bragg. "We did receive an invitation."

"I just don't feel like attending a wedding, Ruthie," said Victor Bragg. "Besides, we hardly know the bride."

"But Marshal Luton is an old friend. We should have gone to his wedding."

"Sarge Luton is not exactly what I would call an old friend, dear. We've known him for years, yes, but we never did actually socialize. We belong to different sets, you know. Hmph. We only just now find out he's alive, and all of a sudden he's getting married—to some divorcee from Texas with a fifteen-year-old son. There's something strange about all this."

"I still think that—"

"I just don't feel up to it. All right?"

"Dearly Beloved," intoned Flagle through his nose, "we are gathered together here in the sight of God and those present to witness the union of this man and this woman in the bonds of Holy Matrimony, which is an honorable estate."

As the preacher droned on, Sarge Luton didn't hear the rest of the words. His eyes and his mind were on Emily. Doc Gallager thought that the entire proceeding was being dragged out most unnecessarily. He wanted to get it over with. The droning continued. Rings were exchanged. Finally Gallager heard the words he had been waiting for. Luton, who was beginning to feel really weak, was also relieved, both for reasons of his physical condition and his anxiety to have the thing done.

"I now pronounce you man and wife," said Flagle. "What God has joined, let no man put asunder. You may now kiss the bride."

Emily turned to face Luton more squarely and she looked up into his eyes. He put his arms around her and touched his lips to hers, briefly and gently. Then Doc Gallager moved in quickly to speed up the process. He didn't want his patient up too long. He shook Luton's hand and congratulated him, then motioned for the others to follow. Reverend Flagle lay in wait for Gallager.

"Who's paying for this, Doc?" he said in a harsh whisper.

Gallager reached into his pocket for cash.

"I'll just add it to my bill," he said.

The last guest to step up to Luton was Oliver Colfax. The two had not met for eight years. They looked at each other for an instant. Colfax put out his hand, and Luton gripped it warmly.

"Congratulations, Sarge," said Colfax. "You've got yourself a fine woman."

"Thank you. Thanks for being here."

Colfax turned to Emily.

"Mrs. Luton," he said, "your husband is the best man I have ever known. I wish you both—all three of you—long life and happiness."

It was the first time Emily had been addressed that way, and she liked the sound of her new name.

"Thank you, Mr. Colfax," she said. "I believe that you've already done more than just wish it for us. You've contributed to our happiness, and perhaps even to our longevity. We appreciate you very much."

Colfax felt his face flush slightly, and he excused himself.

"That's it, folks," said Gallager, suddenly taking charge again. "I've got to get Sarge back in bed—alone."

Chapter Twenty-One

Oliver Colfax had gone to Sergeant Bluff Luton's house and asked Emily for the loan of a suit of Luton's clothes. She had given them to him. It was late evening, and, wearing the borrowed clothing, Colfax sat behind Luton's desk. Luton's hat was pulled down low on Colfax's forehead. On his coat was pinned a star. He had turned the chair around so that his back was to the door, but before him, carefully propped on a shelf on the wall, was a small mirror. In the mirror Colfax could see the front door of the office. There were two armed guards at Doc Gallager's to protect Luton, two more at the Luton home where Emily and Matt were staying, and Colfax knew that across the street, inside an unoccupied office, Blue Steele watched. Leiland Cherry would show up sooner or later. Colfax knew that. He figured that it would be soon.

Just outside of Riddle in the hills to the east, Leiland Cherry sat on a big black stallion. He had just completed a long ride, but the intensity that drove him to finish a job he had long thought to be already accomplished kept up his energy level. Luton would be ready for him this time. The man was no fool. He might be getting old and soft, but Cherry knew his reputation. There had to be a tough and shrewd man behind that reputation. It had been easy the first time. Luton then had not had any reason to expect an attack. But having been shot once, he would be alert, especially since a killing had followed soon afterward and nearby. There were probably special deputies appointed and posted around the town in anticipation of Cherry's arrival. Riddle, he thought, was probably like an armed camp waiting for his invasion. He would not let that stop him, but he would move in cautiously. He would not be caught by surprise.

He eased the big black down to the edge of the hills and over to a small cluster of trees out on the flatland, where he tied the animal out of sight. It was dark enough, Cherry thought, so he began walking toward the town. There was a sudden flash across the night sky, followed by a long, low rumble.

"Dammit," he said, and he walked back to the black and removed a rain slicker from his saddlebags. He slipped on the slicker, then felt of his six-gun beneath it to assure himself of easy access. He would not use the rifle this time. The situation called for sneaking in close. The handgun was preferable. Satisfied, he began the walk again. He had made it about halfway across the open field between the town and the hills when the first drops fell. It was just a sprinkle. He hoped it would not intensify too soon.

Cherry approached Riddle on a back street. Most of the lights were out, so he found it easy to keep to the shadows. His quick eye movements searched out each corner as he moved, each place where deputies might be secreted in the shadows. He knew he was expected. At the corner of the main street and the side street along which he moved, he paused, hugging the building, to look up and down the street for signs of life, signs of danger. He saw no movement, few lights. He did think, however, that one of the lights he could see was probably coming from the marshal's office, but he couldn't be sure because of the angle of his vision. He backtracked, found the alley, and sidled through it until he came to the first lighted building, the one he had decided was the marshal's office. There was an alley window, but a shade was drawn. He could tell only that a light was on in there. There was also a back door. With easy movements Cherry tried the door, only to find it locked. He swore silently to himself, then made his way back around to the street.

Across the street and toward the other end of the block, lights were on in two or three storefronts. They flooded the street at that end of the block, including the sidewalks opposite them, with light. But the end of the block that began where Cherry stood was dark. He calculated that he could get from the corner to the marshal's office without being seen. He took an extra moment to study the street and the storefronts across the street. He saw no signs of life—only the lights. Stepping around the corner, he was startled by the sound of his own boots on the board sidewalk. He stooped to ease them off his feet. Placing the boots there on the sidewalk at the corner, up close to the building, he moved on in his stocking feet. The rain came a little harder.

When Cherry got close to Luton's office, he could see that he would have to pass by a lighted window to reach the door. The space below the window was dark. He would duck under the light of the window to get by. He knew that when he opened the door, he would be caught standing, bathed in light, framed in the doorway. But he figured to get in fast and pull the door shut behind him. He looked around again to reassure himself, then moved on. Just as he had planned, he sneaked under the window. At the door, in shadow again, he stood up, his feet wet from the rain on the boards. He removed the pistol from under the slicker, drew back the hammer, and jerked open the door. He stepped quickly inside, pulling the door shut behind him.

Across the street, Blue Steele saw the light burst forth as the door was opened, saw the framed figure, gun in hand, silhouetted against the bright rectangular backdrop, then watched as the lighted door-frame picture turned to darkness again. He pulled out his Colt, ripped open the door of the office in which he lurked, and ran out into the night toward Luton's office.

Cherry leveled his pistol at the back of the figure sitting behind the desk before him.

"Turn around and watch, Luton," he said.

The figure slowly rotated the office swivel chair until it faced Cherry. It also was holding a gun—a Colt. The Colt was aimed at Cherry's chest.

"Colfax?" said Cherry, astonished. His hesitation cost him his life. Colfax pulled the trigger, and the impact of the slug slammed Cherry back against the door. His face registering disbelief, the gunman sank to his knees. His hand went limp and he dropped his pistol. He stared at Colfax, incredulous. Then his eyes seemed to glaze over, and he fell forward on his face, hitting the hardwood floor with a dull and sickening thud.

Blue Steele hit the door at a run, twisted the knob, and shoved. The door unlatched but met with the resistance of what had been Leiland Cherry on the floor on the other side; it would not swing open.

"Colfax?" he shouted.

"It's okay," said Colfax from inside the office. "It's done."

Doc Gallager released Luton to the custody of his new wife, having given her detailed instructions regarding his care and feeding. When Emily took him outside, Matt was waiting with a buggy to drive them home. Luton climbed gingerly into the buggy with help from both Matt and Emily. He felt a little foolish being pampered like that, but he was still weak and in some pain, and, of course, Emily insisted. As Matt clucked at the horse to set the buggy in motion, Victor Bragg had paused down the street, in front of Clarence Dry's Undertaking Establishment.

There in the front window, on grisly display for all to see, was the body of Leiland Cherry, fully clothed except for his boots, which stood beside him, strapped to a board and propped upright. Bragg paled and hurried away. As the buggy passed by

Victor Bragg, going in the opposite direction, Luton waved at the banker, but he received no acknowledgment. He thought nothing of that, as he had always considered Bragg to be a bit of a stiff-necked snob. The buggy approached Clarence Dry's establishment, and Luton noticed a small crowd beginning to gather there.

"Pull up over there for a minute, Matt," he said. "I bet old Clarence has displayed that man Cherry that Colfax shot. I'd like to get a look at the man who almost did me in."

"Bluff," said Emily, a tone of chastisement in her voice.

"Just a quick look, Emily," he said.

Matt eased the buggy to a halt in front of the window where the crowd stood. One of the curious noticed and spoke to his fellows.

"Hey," he said, "move aside so Sarge can see."

As the crowd parted, they exchanged greetings, congratulations on his marriage and on his recovery, and small talk with Luton. Luton's answers were distracted, though, as his attention was on the body of Leiland Cherry. He stared at it for a long moment. Then he looked away quickly.

"Matt," he said, "drive over to my office."

"Mom?"

Emily looked at Luton, studying the expression on his face.

"Go ahead, Matt," she said.

Inside the marshal's office, Colfax, Miller, and Steele stood around the desk studying a list of names. The name at the top of the list was that of Victor Bragg.

"You'll have to tell me about these people," said Colfax. "I don't know any of them. What about this first one? Bragg. Any reason he's at the top of the list?"

"Just because of his wealth," said Miller. "He owns our bank. He's the richest man around here. You said to make a list of our wealthy citizens, so he was the first one to come to mind."

"Does he travel much?" asked Colfax.

"Why do you ask that?" said Miller.

157

"Because I don't think that most of you people here had ever even heard of Lee Cherry. But a man who travels around some might hear about someone like Cherry."

"Oh. Yes, I suppose so," said Miller. "A business trip every now and then."

"He's got money enough to have hired Lee, and in his travels he might have had the opportunity to learn about him and his trade. Did he stand to gain anything by Sarge's death?"

Miller shook his head.

"I can't imagine anything," he said.

"What about by the death of Lance Fields?" said Steele.

"Well, I—"

Colfax glared at Miller.

"What?" he said.

Miller walked away from the other two men.

"Victor's son, Stan, used to run with Fields," he said. "They got pretty rowdy sometimes, from what I heard."

"That's a fair statement," said Steele. "They usually did it in my town."

"I don't think Victor liked that," Miller continued. "I get the feeling that it upset Ruth—that's Mrs. Bragg—a whole lot. I think Victor blamed it all on the Fields boy."

Blue Steele and Oliver Colfax exchanged glances.

"I got a real strong feeling," said Steele, "that Mr. Bragg didn't want me investigating the Fields murder. He was real uncooperative."

Miller was still off to himself. He stood staring out the back window into the alley. He sighed deeply.

"A short while after Fields was killed," he said, "Stan started back to work in the bank, and back to church with his folks. They were real happy about that—especially Ruth. She came into the store to buy Stan a new suit."

"There's his motive," said Colfax.

"That could explain why Fields was killed," said Miller, "but why was Sarge shot?"

The door of the office came open just then, and Sarge Luton

slowly walked inside, followed closely by Emily and Matt, who helped him to the nearest chair.

"Sarge," said Miller, "should you be up and about like this?"

"It's all right," said Luton. "Doc let me go home, with Emily as my keeper."

"You couldn't have a better one," said Colfax.

Emily's cheeks colored slightly.

"He can only stay a moment," she said. "He does need to get home and back to bed."

"We passed by Clarence Dry's place on the way," said Luton. "He's got that Cherry fellow on display."

"Yes," said Miller, "I know."

"A barbaric practice," said Steele.

"I agree," said Luton. "Barbaric, but maybe useful. I seen him before."

"When?" asked Steele.

"The day before I got shot. He was outside of town with Victor Bragg."

"That's it," said Colfax. "That's all we need. Bragg hired Cherry to kill Fields because he thought that Fields was a bad influence on his kid. But before Cherry went after Fields, Sarge saw him with Bragg. They were afraid that after Cherry had killed Fields, Sarge would put it all together, so they decided to get rid of Sarge first."

"I had suspicions," said Miller. "I didn't want to believe it."

"It's got to be," said Steele.

"Let's go get him," said Colfax, and he headed for the door.

Victor Bragg shut himself in his office at the bank and locked the door. He sat down behind his desk, opened a drawer, and removed a bottle of whiskey and a shot glass. He poured himself a shot and tossed it down in one gulp. Then he poured another. He opened a second drawer and removed a .38 Smith and Wesson revolver, which he placed on his desk before him. Then he took a sip of whiskey. Through the large glass windows of his office he saw the front door of the bank open, then he saw Oliver Colfax enter in a hurry, followed by C. J. Miller and Blue Steele. They were coming toward his office. He picked up the .38, inserted the barrel into his mouth, and pulled the trigger.

Epilogue

Colfax stood on the small front porch of Luton's house. The Lutons and Matt stood facing him.

"Will Milam has always said I could go in with him on his ranch," Luton was saying. "I think maybe I'll resign my job here and go on back to Texas and take him up on that."

"Just as soon as he's strong enough," said Emily.

"Colfax," said Luton, "you could join us down there. It's a big spread. There's always work to be done."

"I don't think so, Sarge," said Colfax. "My reputation would drag you down. I guess I'll go back to the city."

"What'll you do?" said Matt.

"Oh, I'll make out."

Emily put a hand on Colfax's arm.

"I wish you'd reconsider," she said. "You've been a good friend—to all of us."

Colfax looked from the face of one friend to that of another. Here was a family, a family of three. He who had never called anyone friend now had three.

"Well," he said, "you never know. I might."

"Colfax," said Luton, "wherever we go, you'll always be welcome."